The author, Charmian Coates who lives in Bla⌐¹ ', was born in Ilford, Essex, in 1937. Aged ⌐' ⌐n to India and spent two-and-⌐ ' ired her to write her fii ⌐ is a widow with one ⌐d. Neil, her second so⌐ ⌐s completely helpless. ⌐. She also has five ⌐ great-grandchildren.

In 1972, she left ⌐₁ᵤ to run alongside her late husband, Alan, a small private hotel in Blackpool. This novel, 'G.I. Bridegroom' was inspired by her late brother-in-law, Reg, who was a navigator on a Lancaster Bomber in WW2.

Charmian has had several novels published by Pegasus, and a childrens' novel published by Authorhouse.

Last year, 2013, she was awarded a B.A. Hons in Creative Writing from the University of Creative Art, at the Royal Festival Hall, London.

G. I. BRIDEGROOM

CHARMIAN COATES

Published by New Generation Publishing in 2014

First Edition

www.newgeneration-publishing.com

New Generation Publishing

Dedicated to the memory of my late brother-in-law,
Harold Montague Reginald (Reg)Coates,

A navigator on a Lancaster Bomber in WW2
1920 - 1990

ONE OF THE BRAVE

ACKNOWLEDGEMENTS

With grateful thanks to my son, Reg, daughter-in law, Caroline, and granddaughter, Sarah for all her care.

Also, thanks to good friends, Jacki Buksh and Mary Cardwell (Sis).

Thanks too, to Mary Cardwell, and my partner, Ronnie Pennington for their helpful suggestions.

And finally, I'd like to mention the Lancashire Authors Association of which I've been a member since 1994.

CHAPTER ONE

'Brumm... Brumm...,' went the engines of the Lancaster bomber, as it flew, resembling a giant blackbird with monstrous outstretched wings, through the dark sky on its latest mission to Germany. Flying too, alongside, like a shadowy flock of birds, and loudly pulsating, were many other bombers. They reached the target where their bombs were to be dropped, being attacked all around them by flak from the ground below. Suddenly, the bomb-aimer, at the front of the plane shouted, "Hell! The bomb doors are stuck!"

Roger Bowler, the plane's navigator, in the seat nearest to the bomb-aimer, got up, grabbed a hatchet nearby which was there in case of an emergency, and unsteadily made his way towards the bomb doors. He was shaking, his forehead sticky beneath his flying helmet; should the plane find an air pocket and jerk when he'd levered open the doors, he could lose his balance and fall through them to certain death. He got the doors open, at the same moment, the plane jerked, he almost did lose his balance, but just saving himself in time by throwing down the hatchet and desperately grabbing hold of the bomb-rack.

The bombs were successfully dropped over Berlin, whining like banshees as they fell onto the city below. Relieved, through lightening skies, they headed back to Blighty and their airfield.

As he climbed down from the plane, he thought, well, I've not been killed tonight, but I may be on my next mission, or the one after.

* * *

Eighteen-year-old Susan Swift looked admiringly at the living room table which was covered with a snow white cloth and laden with plates of sandwiches. These sandwiches were draped with dampened tea towels to keep

1

the sandwiches fresh. There was also plates of sausage rolls, cheese straws, fancy cakes and jam tarts, the tarts filled with home-made blackberry jam. Susan had gone with Alec, her new fiancé Roger's younger brother, the previous autumn to pick the fruit at Shotover Common, Headington, and Roger's mother, Mrs Bowler, her mother-in- law- to- be had made the jam. She got on well with middle-aged Mrs Bowler, who at only 4ft 9" was as round as a barrel, with light brown hair, the colour of Roger's own, which was worn in a bun at the back of her neck. Usually, she wore a wrap-around apron; it seemed strange to see her dressed in her best dress. She had told Susan she'd bought the striped material from the cattle market which was held every Wednesday at the Ox pens, near the station. As well as the pens where the animals were kept before they were auctioned, there were stalls where fruit and vegetables, meat and fish, and also curtaining and dress materials were sold. This had been some years previously. She had then made up the dress herself on her Singer Sewing Machine which she'd had since she was in Service before the Great War. She'd also used the machine to run up most of her sons' clothing when they were small, her late father-in-law, Mr Bowler senior had been a tailor who used to sit cross-legged on the floor to do his sewing. He'd given her newspaper patterns that he'd cut out for her to make the little trousers for her boys. Susan's attention turned to Mr Bowler who was attired in his best suit; at around 5ft 6", unlike his wife, he was spare in build, and had curly dark brown hair with only a few grey ones in it. Mr and Mrs Bowler had no daughters, only three sons (Wilfred at sixteen was five years younger than Roger and was apprenticed to a plumber, and their youngest son, Alec, was eight years Roger's junior and thirteen) and Susan knew that Mrs Bowler was only too pleased to welcome her into the family as a daughter.

She'd told her that she's always wanted one. Her own mother and Mrs Bowler had been baking for days to work this minor miracle, especially with the rationing. In the centre of the spread was a small white iced cake, a combined twenty-first birthday and engagement cake.

She reached for Roger's hand and as she did so, the small diamond glittered in the ring he'd recently presented her with. She squeezed his hand in excitement. He squeezed hers in return.

He was so handsome in his R.A.F. uniform and she felt certain that other girls must envy her.

It was the 8th of June. The year was 1941, and Roger Bowler was home on leave from the R.A.F. which he had joined at the outbreak of war in 1939. Home was a three-bedroomed terraced house in a street with no front gardens at Osney Island, Oxford, which was near to Oxford Station and this party was to celebrate his twenty-first birthday as well as his engagement to Susan, who was three years his junior. They had known each other since she was fifteen when she would ride on her bicycle to his house, her fair pigtails flying, still in her school uniform; she had won a scholarship to Milham Ford, a prestigious grammar school. Her parents, Mr and Mrs Swift were now close friends with Roger's own parents.

They came regularly of a Friday evening to play cards.

Susan looked around the room. A wooden sideboard with a runner across its top boasted dozens of framed family pictures as did the mantelpiece over the black-leaded range which had an oven at one side, on the hob of which, a big blackened kettle was always simmering. Two elderly armchairs were draped with faded curtains. As well as the armchairs there were a dozen hard-backed chairs, several of them having been collected up from the bedrooms so there would be enough seats for the visitors.

"When can we start on the food," remarked Alec, his colouring similar to Roger's own who was hovering near the table and licking his lips, "I'm hungry."

Mrs Bowler, entering the room with another plate of sandwiches overheard him. "You always are."

"Well, I'm growing, Mum."

"That's true, I suppose. Won't be long now before we

3

eat, you'll have to be patient. "

Alec's face fell.

There was a knock on the door. "That'll be some more guests. "Let them in, will you, Susan?"

She went to open it. On the step were all their friends of a similar age to themselves from the New Road Baptist chapel; her best friend, Angela whose short curly hair was as dark as Susan's was fair and whom she had known since Infant School, and Roger's friend Lionel, whom he'd known since Grammar School. "Come in, come in," she exclaimed.

In they came and crowded into the living room, most of them with parcels in their hands. There was a further knock and several of Roger's uncles and aunts on Roger's dad's side appeared. His mother's side all lived too far away to attend the party. Fortunately, thought Susan, as they were packed like sardines in a can as it was. Last to arrive was her parents. Taking piled plates of food, the younger guests retired to the front room, where on a table were already dozens of engagement presents, such as saucepans, tea towels and other necessary items for when Susan and Roger would be married and about to set up home together, while the older guests, including Susan's parents settled themselves on the hard-backed chairs in the living room.

With Alec proudly wearing his first pair of long trousers and seated on the floor (there weren't enough seats for everyone) and Wilfred (his colouring resembling his father's) he, looking rather bored (obviously, he would have rather been out with his mates than at his elder brother's party) soon all the guests were tucking in, none more so than Alec, leaving nothing but crumbs on the plates.

"Do you want to cut the cake now?" asked Mrs Bowler, popping her head around the front room door.

Everyone returned to the living room where Susan and Roger then cut the engagement cake to cheers. But the thing that got the biggest cheer was when Roger's dad came in with a large cardboard key covered in silver paper that he had made in the Railway Workshops where he worked. Everyone then sung:

"Twenty-one today, twenty- one today.

He's got the key of the door, never been twenty-one before..."

After the party, Roger walked Susan home. Her parents were still at his house, her mother, Mrs Swift was helping his mother, Mrs Bowler to clear away and wash up. They entered the two bedroomed terraced house which was only a few streets away. The narrow passage was draped with coats which hung from hooks on the wall. He eagerly pulled her to him and gave her a passionate kiss. She kissed him back. At this, greatly daring, he touched her breast and tried to undo the buttons of her blouse. He felt her respond, but then she pulled away. "Don't do that!"

He paused. "Why not, you want me, don't you? I want you."

"I know you do, and I do as well, but..."

He pulled her to him again. "You do love me, don't you?"

"Of course I do."

"Then let me. I love you and we're engaged now. Most couples don't wait for the wedding ring to enjoy lovemaking once they are engaged. All the friends I have made at the RAF camp say that their fiancée's allow them intimacies."

Susan's lip trembled. "They might, but I can't! And what if I was to get pregnant? It'd be such a disgrace. My parents, and yours too, I'm certain, would be devastated. Oh, I know you would do the decent thing by me, and I do want babies but not yet. I certainly don't want to have to get married."

"I've got something to prevent a baby." He removed a small packet from his pocket.

She blushed. "Put it away. That's disgusting!"

He hastily did just that.

And if you loved me" she continued. "You wouldn't

expect me to give in to you. You know, as well as I do that it's a sin. We've both been taught that at Chapel."

"I know, but..."

"Come on. At least, let's get into the living room." She pushed him towards it.

"There's a good programme on the wireless." Entering the room which was almost identical to his parents' living room, she indicated one of the armchairs. "Just sit down there and I'll make us a cup of tea and we can listen to it."

* * *

Later, as he walked back home, Roger felt so disappointed. He reckoned he was the only one at his camp in Lincolnshire who was still a virgin. He'd hoped to rectify this now they were engaged. Fat chance! He'd not told Susan of the danger he was in when he went on the 'ops over Germany, he didn't want her to worry, but all the same he didn't want to die before he had enjoyed what all the other lads he knew seemed to be enjoying. Susan said things would be different between them once they were married, even so, that was ages away.

Mr Swift wouldn't give his permission before Susan was twenty-one for her to marry. She was about to leave school and was hoping for a job as a shorthand typist in an office. With her salary and what he earned as a navigator on the Lancaster bombers they could save up and so start off their married life far more easily than either of their parents had. But as far as the physical side of marriage went, would everything be okay? With her refusing him she could be a cold fish. There were some girls who were like that or so he'd heard. Passing the Old Gate Public House he decided to go in there to drown his sorrows.

* * *

"You're very quiet today," remarked Angela, as the two girls rode their bicycles home from Milham Ford School.

"I'd have thought you would have been bubbling up with excitement now that you're engaged?"

They reached Susan's house. "I am, I suppose, but..."

"But, what?"

Susan flushed. "It is rather personal..."

"Surely you can tell me? We've known each other for years."

Susan made up her mind. "Come in for a bit and I'll tell you what's bothering me. We won't be overheard; Mum'll be out at Chapel, her Mother's Union meeting."

They parked their bicycles against the house wall in the pocket-sized front garden and went inside. They climbed the oil-cloth covered stairs and entered Susan's bedroom. Against one wall stood a large oak wardrobe, and against the other was a matching wash-hand-stand covered by a white crocheted-edged runner, on top of which was a white china basin and jug.

The floor was covered with linoleum and at the side of the bed which wasn't against the wall was a brightly coloured rag-rug that Mrs Swift had made herself. The window had blackout curtains that would be drawn once it went dark. They seated themselves side by side on top of the pale pink eiderdown on Susan's bed. "So what is it?" asked Angela gently. "Is it because Roger has returned to his camp? You're missing him?"

"I am, of course. No, it isn't that, though of course I'll miss him, "Susan replied shakily. "After the party last night, well, Roger tried to make love to me."

"He did what!!"

"I wanted to as well, but..."

Angela frowned. "That'd be a sin. And if you should become pregnant, oh, that would be terrible. If Roger refused to do the right thing by you, and your parents wouldn't stand by you, you could end up in a Mother and Baby Home."

"I know."

"I've heard some tales about those homes. Treat the girls like dirt, work them like slaves and even knock them about. Then they coerce them into giving up the babies for adoption. Fancy never seeing your own little baby ever again. That'd be awful."

"Terrible!

"Could scar you for life," added Angela.

"But anyway, I couldn't let him. I just couldn't."

"Good thing, too, how did he take it?"

"I don't think he was best pleased. He said all the fellows he knows on his camp are making love to their fiancée's. And that now we are engaged, I should let him."

"Cheek! Anyway, that's what they tell him, it doesn't necessarily follow that it's true."

"Maybe not, Angela, but what if he should look elsewhere. He told me I was a prude."

"Better to be a prude than pregnant."

Susan's bottom lip trembled. "You're right, of course. Still, there are a lot of young WAAF's at his camp. They probably haven't got the same principals as me. He told me once that they call these girls 'the Officer's Ground-Sheets'.

Angela laughed. "I shouldn't worry about them. Surely he wouldn't want a girl that isn't fussy who she sleeps with?"

"I don't know. I really don't know."

They heard the front door open, followed by footsteps. "Shush! That'll be Mum," whispered Susan immediately changing the subject to that of the homework they needed to do for the following morning.

CHAPTER TWO

Roger walked to the phone box carrying his case. His leave was over and he was due back at camp. He dialled the taxi number and when someone answered he pressed Button A. "I'm ringing from the phone box by Whites the Greengrocers, can I have a taxi immediately to the station?"

"Certainly, sir," said a voice from the other end of the line.

Though it was less than a five minute walk from his house to Oxford Station, he always arrived there by taxi. He had two mates who were also stationed with him, and lived in big houses at North Oxford and whose fathers were middle- class business men, unlike his own working class father. He didn't want them to realise where he lived, which was a working class area. If they knew they might look down on him. Though he guessed their middle-class girlfriends were the worst when it came to class prejudice, women were always worse than men when it came to something like that.

Unlike the majority of boys he had known since childhood, he had won a scholarship at eleven and been educated at the grammar school where he had stayed until he was sixteen after which he had obtained a position at Rumble and Badstocks, an estate agents in Cornmarket. He had paid for elocution lessons to obtain a more upper class accent. After a few lessons his dad had enquired whenever they passed the time of day together, whether he had a plum in his mouth. All the same, the elocution lessons had stood him in good stead when he was accepted for training in Bomber Command.

The taxi duly arrived and he climbed in. Seconds later, he was at his destination. He paid the taxi driver his fare and alighted. As he stood on the crowded platform waiting for his train, he wondered whether he would ever see this station again, with its out-of-action cigarette and chocolate machines, or would his next 'op see him shot down and killed like so many of those he'd known at RAF Henswell. He had found all this death difficult to come to terms with, especially when the following day after an 'op there were so many missing faces.

He mulled over the events of the last few months. The briefing and debriefing before and after an 'op was done by Wing Commander Collins, a rather stuffy middle-aged man with a balding head. Behind him was a huge map of Germany, and at the side of him, a blackboard.

Before an 'op he pointed out with a long cane the area of Germany they were to bomb, then he wrote instructions in chalk on the blackboard. Everyone, like himself, seated before him with butterflies in their stomachs, caused by a mixture of excitement and terror. It was left to the aircrew themselves to sort out which bomber they would crew. The take-off time for an 'op could be any time of the day, depending on the weather, though ninety per cent of operations were at night, flying over enemy territory in the dark, dependant on maps and instruments, aware that enemy fighters would be on their tail. They flew manually and "rolled" the 37 ton loaded plane to see if any enemy fighters were underneath them. The take-off time was a secret until they were ordered to report for duty. He recalled being woken by his batman and told 'Briefing in fifty minutes', sir."

On quite a few occasions, he and the rest of the crew would receive a radio message while on a training flight. Sometimes, with everyone ready in position, the green light which told you to take off was replaced by a red one, telling them their operation had been cancelled. What a relief that was to be able to take off the flying kit (this was necessary as it was fifty degrees below freezing in the rear turret) and which took an hour to put on and go back to bed and know that you wouldn't die that night. The two eggs on your plate which was the usual breakfast for everyone on return from a mission wasn't a big enough temptation to risk your life for. Though, these days with the bombing anyone could die anywhere. His thoughts moved on to the devastation of so many English towns and cities by the Luftwaffe. How awful it would be to come home on leave and find your home demolished and all your family dead. So far Oxford had been lucky and not been bombed, some said this was because so many of the Nazis had been educated at the Oxford Colleges and wanted to keep them undamaged. Or it could be that Oxford was in a misty hollow and could not be seen from the air. But you never really knew. There was only one occasion when it looked as if they were about to join all those other cities that had been devastated. It was when gas cylinders and bottles exploded at the lemonade factory at the other side of the river that ran alongside East Street. It had certainly put the wind up quite a few people as cylinders came whistling above their heads. The subsequent fire at the factory had lit up the nearby Electric Light Works.

There'd been rumours of saboteurs...

He felt a friendly thump on his arm. "If it isn't old Roger, the dodger," laughed a familiar voice. It was Ben with whom he shared his accommodation at Henswell, "Dodger, yourself," he retorted.

"Don't be like that; you know you love me really."

"Huh!"

Stocky-built, of medium height, dark-haired, and with a brown handlebar moustache, Ben was okay; he was always good for a laugh as he didn't take life too seriously. They needed something or someone to lighten their mood with the thoughts of what they had experienced over Germany so many times, and would need to experience again and again, if they weren't killed before this war was over. A skinful of ale weren't enough. Stood next to Ben with a big grin on his face was Charlie. Both men were navigators like himself. Six-feet tall and as a skinny as a telegraph pole, Charlie was red-haired and freckled. He certainly had the gift of the gab as regards the girls. He was well known as a womaniser amongst the WAAFS stationed at the camp, and Roger imagined he had broken quite a few hearts. "So did you get engaged to Susan, that's your girl's name, isn't it?"

"Yes, Susan and I got engaged."

"Congratulations," said Ben, putting out his hand to shake Roger's.

Charlie looked mournful. "Tying yourself to one girl when there are so many gorgeous girls about is daft."

"That's your opinion, it isn't mine."

"Look what you are missing."

"One of those sexual deceases?" suggested Roger.

Charlie laughed. "I'm too careful. And did she let you have it?"

"Leave him alone, you're embarrassing the lad," put in Ben.

Roger reddened. Err...of course." It was a lie but how could he admit the truth, that he was still a virgin. He thought of Daisy, a little WAAF with whom he had chatted when he and his mates were in the Mess drinking themselves stupid or playing leap frog. She was a cuddly little blonde and had made it obvious that she had taken quite a fancy to him. Daisy was employed in the Operations Room where he knew they had to be very quick in placing the arrows down when locating the enemy aircraft as they came over. Would her response be equally as quick when it came to giving him what he so desperately wanted? He felt hot all over at the thought of it. And if it was, could he cheat on Susan? Did he really love her? He wasn't sure. Perhaps he had known her too long, or it could be that his eyes had been opened since he'd joined the RAF, and he wanted a more exciting girl than one who only expected to work for a while before marriage and then be satisfied with looking after a home and bringing up a family.

"I hope she isn't in the club now? Did you use a rubber?" said Charlie.

With effort Roger dragged his thoughts away from what he might enjoy with little Daisy. "Err...Do you think

12

I'm daft...?"

His words were lost as the train roared in surrounded by clouds of white smoke.

Everyone, mostly servicemen, humping their luggage, surged towards it. He and his mates tried to find a compartment that they could squeeze into but it was hopeless, they were all already crowded with passengers, so they had to sit on their cases in the packed corridor.

Doors banged, the Station Master blew his whistle. The train shuddered, its wheels beginning to turn. It speeded up, rattling and jerking, taking them nearer all the time to Lincolnshire and their destiny.

* * *

After their arrival at the camp and a quick wash and brush up, Roger and his mates spent the evening in the smoky atmosphere of the Mess, in which someone playing on the piano was singing drunkenly the rousing chorus of a popular nonsense song:

"Mairzy doats and dozy doats and liddle lamsey divey.
A kiddley divey too, wouldn't you...?"

Above the pianist on the top of the piano was a pint of beer and next to it in an ashtray smouldered a lighted cigarette. As well as the musical entertainment, darts and snooker as well as card games were in progress, not to mention, a game of leap frog. The noise was deafening, with dozens of conversations being carried on at once and raucous laughter fuelled by alcohol. Then to Roger's delight he found that little Daisy was present, seated at one of the circular wooden tables.

"Do you want a game of darts?" asked Charlie.

Then he noticed where and whom Roger was intent on. Charlie looked at Ben and winked. "Roger fancies a different game to darts." Both men laughed.

Roger moved towards Daisy.

Her eyes lit up as she recognised him. "Hello, Roger," she said shyly.

He smiled at her. "Can I get you a drink?" he offered.

"Port-and-lemon, please," she replied.

He went up to the bar for their drinks. After quite some time, the area around the bar being packed, he managed to get served.

She sipped hers. "Have you been on leave?" she asked, "I haven't seen you in here lately."

He nodded. "Yes, I've been home – to Oxford," he added. He never mentioned what he had been doing while he was there – getting engaged.

"I've always wanted to visit Oxford – see all those colleges that are hundreds of years old," she said wistfully. "The sights they must have seen, the clever men of learning that must have been taught within them. I wonder if our present Prime Minister, Winston Churchill could have studied there. "

"I don't know." Roger wasn't interested in Winston Churchill; he was more interested in the way Daisy's uniform skirt was riding up to reveal her slim legs as she perched on top of a wooden stool.

He made up his mind. "Would you like to come to the pictures with me one evening when I'm not on call, there's a good film on in Lincoln which came out only recently, 'Penny Serenade' starring Cary Grant and Irene Dunne?" If they were cuddled up together in the back row of the cinema and sharing a few kisses, he wondered if she would push away a wandering hand?

Her eyes brightened. "I've heard of `Penny Serenade', it's a romance, isn't it?"

"I believe so."

"How will we get to Lincoln?

"I'll take you there on my motorbike." He had purchased the Norton three months earlier from his friend, Lionel, Lionel having bought a newer, larger model. His parents kept the Swan pub at Cowley, and Lionel was their only child, so consequently he was spoiled and given everything he wanted. He was a good mate though, and also a keen river fisherman.

When they could, Lionel was also in the RAF but stationed at a different camp, they would go fishing together. Roger didn't eat the fish he'd caught from the River Thames (though once he had fried up an eel in a frying pan for his supper) but took them home for Tiger, the family's tortoiseshell cat to supplement the animal's diet of rabbit which Roger's mother would boil up for him. But Tiger's favourite snacks (all the houses on Osney Island were overrun with mice) could be heard squeaking from behind the wainscoting – should one venture out, Tiger would leap on it, and seconds later, be sitting back washing his whiskers with satisfaction. Susan didn't like Roger going fishing with Lionel, she didn't approve of him, didn't really approve of any of Roger's friends. Perhaps that was one of the reasons that he was cooling towards her. He wasn't going to be dominated by Susan the way that Susan's father was.

"It will be straight there, and straight back?" she replied archly.

Roger laughed. "You'll have to wait and see."

* * *

It was a warm evening when they drove to Lincoln for their cinema trip. Firstly they'd to sit through news of the war, which wasn't exactly cheering. At last the big film began.

Daisy seemed to enjoy it, though, he himself would have preferred something not so soppy. A cowboy film with lots of fisticuffs and shooting would have been more to his taste. Under the cover of darkness, he placed an arm around her shoulder, pulling her closer. She made no objection and had laid her head on his shoulder. Encouraged by her response, he then attempted a few kisses which, to his delight, she returned enthusiastically.

The film ended and after singing the National Anthem

alongside all the other cinema goers, they left the cinema and found his motorbike which he had parked nearby.

With her sitting behind him on the pillion with her arms tightly around his waist, they set off for the camp. Half way there, as they drove along a secluded country road, chuckling under his breath, he turned off the petrol. A few hundred yards along the road the engine spluttered and died. "What's wrong with your bike, Roger?" she asked, concerned, as the bike slowed and stopped and they got off it.

"Nothing to worry about, it's done it before. The engine just needs to cool down. It will be okay soon. Let's sit on the grass for a while and wait for it to do that," he suggested.

She frowned, but she obediently seated herself down on the grass.

He did the same. "I'm whacked," he exclaimed, and he lay down on his back.

She nodded. "All those 'ops must take it out of you."

"They do. Look at those lovely white clouds up above."

She changed her position from sitting to lying. "You're right. There's one that looks like a snowy mountain."

"Is there?" He wasn't really interested in clouds, he saw enough of them when flying, but agreed, then putting his arms about her; he drew her closer, their lips met in kisses which became more and more heated. He ran a hand up her leg and fingered the flesh above her stocking top. He caressed her body, undoing the buttons of her uniform blouse to release her breasts. He toyed with her nipples which grew hard beneath his fingertips. He had got as far as trying to ease her knickers down when she suddenly said, "No!"

He paused. "What do you mean, no," he replied in disbelief, "You want it, don't you?"

"Yes, but not yet." She readjusted her clothing. "We were going too far. I want to wait until I am married to go all the way."

"That's old fashioned having to wait until you're

married. No one else does it these days, especially with the war on."

"I don't care if it is, that's what I'm determined upon."

"If that's what you want there is no more to be said." Swallowing his disappointment, he got to his feet and taking her hand, pulled her up off the ground.

Daisy's lip trembled. "You're not cross, are you, Roger?"

"No, of course not, how could anyone ever be cross with a sweet little thing like you."

She looked relieved.

They got back on the motorbike and with a few sharp kicks from Roger, it roared into life. Soon they were approaching the camp .He wouldn't give up on her yet. He would ask Daisy out again, maybe with a bit of effort on his part he could break down her resolve.

CHAPTER THREE

Shaking slightly from the cold as well as nerves, Roger and the rest of his crew, Pilot, Flight Engineer, Wireless Operator, Bomb Aimer, Mid Upper Gunner and the Rear Gunner, approached their Lancaster. Suddenly, Bert, the Wireless Operator bent and kissed the ground. "Don't forget this is only au revoir, not goodbye!"

He rose. Roger, laughing, grabbed hold one of Bert's arms, and John, the Tail Gunner, grabbed the other and with much hilarity, they pushed him up the ladder and into the bomber.

This laughter somehow diminished the tension they were all feeling; a team of seven men, who felt cut off from the rest of the world, with a job to do before they could return to earth.

They weren't the only ones with a job to do, so were the two homing pigeons chirping merrily in their cage; pigeons were used to send a message back to base should they have to ditch their plane into the sea. Take-off was always a tense moment because any engine trouble at such a time could be serious, especially with the bombs aboard. Luckily, everything was perfect and as soon as they were airborne everyone relaxed and settled down for a long trip into darkness.

An hour after take-off they were flying at about 12,000 feet, on course to Berlin. Like a monster blackbird searching for a perch, the Lancaster glided through the sky. They flew on for three hours, all quiet and undisturbed, except for a few searchlights which tried to pierce the thick cloud below. The flak over the coastline was completely visible. They were now flying in a clear sky lit by searchlights, fighter flares and explosions above the suburbs of Berlin. Roger, from his navigating calculations could see they were eight to ten minutes behind the correct bombing time. This couldn't be helped though and the bombs were released, falling with a whine to the suburbs below like giant hailstones. Then what every member of the crew always dreaded happening to them, happened to Bert. He was caught short and had to relief himself sitting aft on the chemical Elsen toilet. A bursting bladder, or erupting bowel was no joke while heading through the sky over enemy territory. Men had died on the lav' when their aircraft had been hit. This time though, fortunately, it wasn't Bert's time to die.

On the way home, crossing the North Sea they met Dormiers and Heinkels, 300 to 400 yards from them, going the other way, the Luftwaffe having bombed England. These planes just ignored them, it wasn't their business to engage the enemy. Neither was it that of the R.A.F., whose job it was to simply drop their bombs and return to base. Crossing the English Channel, as usual, Thermos flasks filled with tea were eagerly produced and Roger took a satisfying swig from his. "Tastes better even than beer," he announced.

There were grunts of agreement from the other crew members. After wearing oxygen masks for long hours everyone's mouth was parched and dry. Lincolnshire was covered in thick fog. Their aircraft hit something, lurched, went over it at an angle, then struck something else and landed the other way. Because of the fog, Roger didn't know at the time that with 500 feet showing on the altimeter and all engines going full pelt, they'd hit the ground. The two obstructions were ditches which had torn off the undercarriage legs. The Lancaster roared across several fields before coming to a sudden jolting halt. The four engines literally fell out of the wings and the propellers screwed themselves into the ground. Everyone hurriedly climbed out, thinking about fire. Almost immediately, they were picked up by RAF transport and taken back to camp, where, after debriefing, the room thick with cigarette smoke, and in which copious cups of black coffee were needed to keep them awake, they fell exhausted into their beds.

The next morning, after eating his two egg breakfast in

the Mess, Roger studied the letter beside his plate which had arrived from Susan.

'Dearest Roger,

I do hope everything is all right with you, that you are safe and well. I think of you all the time and look forward to when you next have some leave and come home to Oxford. But I've got some great news. I shall be able see you before that as Mother and I are coming up next week to Lincolnshire on the train for a couple of days and stopping at the post office in the village near your camp. Do you think you will be able to get some time off so that you can take us around? '

He went cold all over and his eyes blurred so that he could hardly take in the rest of her letter. It might seem good news for her but it wasn't for him! Making an effort, he tried to focus on the next sentence.

'I have been for an interview for a secretarial post at the solicitors, Berry and Brown, but there was a couple of other applicants, all the same I still hope to get the position...'

What was he going to do? He had taken Daisy out several more times since that first occasion, for walks and to the pictures, and he knew he was beginning to break down her resolve to keep him at arms-length. The next time he tried it on with her he felt sure he would get his own way. But now, though he didn't really want to, he would have to finish with her, it was too risky not to. He couldn't let Susan, and more particularly, Susan's mother, who was something of a tartar, know about Daisy. He couldn't risk someone inadvertently letting something slip should they meet up with them in the village. If Susan's mother should realise he had been playing around when he was engaged to her daughter, she would probably tell his parents. Being rather narrow minded, they would be shocked at something like this, especially as he knew they were very fond of Susan. He'd have to finish with Daisy, he had no choice. He didn't like doing this, but what else could he do? He wanted to let her down lightly, but how? The answer to his problem suddenly came to him as he recalled Bert being caught short recently while they were airborne. It could have been him sitting on that Elsen and the plane getting hit and consequently, being killed. That was it, he'd keep well away from the Mess, and when Daisy asked where he was, she could be told by Charlie that he had caught a bullet on their recent 'op, Charlie was the best choice, he was sure he would do it, he would think it a fantastic prank. There might be a few tears from Daisy at the news that he was no more, but she hadn't known him that long, given time she should get over it okay and be able to carry on with her life. Yes, that was what he would do, he decided.

* * *

As Roger had expected Charlie agreed to do the dirty deed. "Perhaps I can console her," he'd added with a laugh.

That evening, instead of going to the Mess with the others Roger had stayed behind in their room, lying on his bed and attempting to read a Hank Jansen book.

A few hours later, Charlie returned; the worse for wear as usual. He flopped onto his bed and began to snore.

Roger poked him in the chest. "Wake up!"

"Whada want?" mumbled Charlie, trying to push him away.

"How did she take it?" said Roger, somewhat shamefaced.

"Who?"

"Daisy, of course."

"The little WAAF?"

Roger swallowed. "Yes, was she very upset?"

"What do you think," replied Charlie. "She burst into tears and ran out of the Mess. She didn't even wait to let me console her, a real pity that was. I would have given her an experience she would never forget. "Now, let me get to sleep, I'm jiggered."

The next day Roger heard that Daisy had asked to be transferred immediately to another camp. He sighed with relief at the news. It was just after Susan and her mother had visited him, their visit going off without any hitch, that another pretty little WAAF was transferred to their camp. Her name was Myrtle, and her hair was a rich chocolate brown.

Charlie had spotted her too. "I reckon she's a 'goer'. She's got a glint in her eye. I'd be in there myself if I hadn't already got two girls on the go. It's not easy, I can tell you, keeping both of them happy without either of them finding out about the other."

Roger didn't know anything about glints or 'goers', but he couldn't resist chatting Myrtle up himself. He knew he should have learnt his lesson after Daisy, but he still hoped that with Myrtle being a 'goer' she would allow him what both Susan and Daisy hadn't. This time, he decided not to take the girl for a ride on his motorbike and the flicks. He'd take her to the village pub instead, loosen her reservations with several glasses of port-and-lemon; put it on thick as to how he was so attracted to her.

All went well, Myrtle agreed to go out with him. The following evening, they set off for the village pub. The Plough had a thatched roof, and inside, the ceiling were bare rafters. On the walls were hung farming implements. The atmosphere was thick with smoke due to a group of elderly pipe-smoking regulars who were playing dominoes. They looked up and shot them a disapproving stare before returning to their game. Myrtle seated herself at a well-worn circular table while Roger fetched their drinks from the bar. The middle-aged landlord; sleeves rolled to his elbows had wispy white hair and a drinker's nose and cheeks which were covered with red-thread veins, served him. Seated with their drinks, he then went to work on her. Soon, she was giggling at his flattery as she downed several brimming glassfuls of port-and lemon. So far, so good, he thought as he escorted her from the pub and down a lonely country lane. He pulled her to him, and his mouth closed on hers. She seemed to enjoy it, so encouraged, he went further, attempting to undo the buttons on her shirt. Suddenly, she was deadly sober. "What do you think you're doing?" With this, she gave him a mighty shove and losing his balance he fell, on top of a very soft cow pat.

He got up, twisted around and registered that the seat of his trousers was completely covered in stinking brown muck. But the worst thing of all was that Myrtle was holding her nose and hysterically laughing at him.

Feeling ridiculous, Roger gave her a black look, all thoughts of getting his way with her forgotten. They walked back to the camp in silence. .After this, whenever he should see her in the Mess, embarrassed, he looked the other way. He only hoped that she hadn't told anyone how he had been made to look a fool.

Myrtle and the cow pat were forgotten, when a few days later, he and Charlie heard they were to be sent to America to train as pilots. America! Roger couldn't believe it, his head being full of Hollywood and film stars and the wonderful lifestyle that they were about to experience.

CHAPTER FOUR

Roger and Charlie travelled by train to Liverpool. Seeing all the destruction near the docks, although Roger knew all about the bombing of cities and towns from the wireless and the newspapers, as well as the Pathe News at the cinema, it still shocked him to see what was once peoples' homes, laid waste. Waiting to embark, they stood on the dockside looking up at the ship they were to travel to America on.

Charlie rubbed the crick in the back of his neck. "It's huge. Longer that our street."

"I've never been on the ocean before," confessed Roger.

"You're not the only one," replied Charlie. "I hope I don't get seasick."

"Me, neither."

Roger had seen the sea before. Several times, over the years before the war, he had travelled by train to Barry Island with his parents and two younger brothers and stopped in a guest house for a week. He recalled paddling in the sea, donkey rides across the sands, and watching Punch and Judy shows. Working for the railway, his dad got several free railway passes a year. Sometimes, before Wilfred and Alec had been born they'd just gone to the seaside for the day with sandwiches and a flask of tea. He thought of Susan's reaction when he had gone home on leave and told her that he was about to leave England for a few months. There had been floods of tears which he'd found embarrassing, and he had to promise he wouldn't be tempted by the American girls in their Bermuda shorts and bobby socks that they had seen in so many films from the back row of the Ritz Cinema.

His mother too, he knew, hadn't been too happy either about him going so far away. She was concerned about the ship he would sail on being torpedoed by German submarines as so many other ships had been.

Alec though, had thought it all very exciting. He seemed to imagine, having seen too many Westerns that Roger once he reached America would be toting a gun, riding a horse, lassoing cattle and sleeping in a bunk house with cowboys, despite his explanation that he would be nowhere near the Wild West.

They embarked, not only Roger and Charlie, but a dozen or more RAF personnel from other camps who were also going to America to be trained as pilots. Unfortunately, they'd suffered rough weather on the voyage with seas higher than mountains that threatened to swamp the ship. Both Roger and Charlie suffered badly from seasickness, lying in their bunks and holding brown paper bags beneath their chins. Fortunately, though, they saw no sign of any German submarines. That was one new experience that Roger didn't want to have – of ending up in a lifeboat if he was lucky, or if he wasn't, floating for hours in the freezing sea – that's if he lasted that long!

Six days later they arrived at St John's, Newfoundland, after which they travelled by train to Montgomery, Alabama. The heat hit them; it was so much warmer than England, though everywhere electric fans whirred. They were well looked after during training. At the camp in Montgomery they repeated their basic training as it was an American camp. The food was far more plentiful to what they were used to. They were offered a staggering choice for breakfast. They eventually settled for bacon and two eggs each. One of the others asked for seven eggs and got them – thinking him greedy and showing the British up in a bad light, everyone made sure he cleared his plate. They weren't allowed off the base for six weeks, but when they were finally let out they were allowed to wear civilian clothes as the U.S.A. was not in the war. There they made the acquaintance of drugstores, from which not only medicines could be obtained but also frothy milkshakes in different flavours. But the thing that struck him the most was so many black faces everywhere; he'd hardly ever seen one in Oxford, and he was shocked by the way these

Negroes were treated by the white population – separate restaurants, buses and schools. He wasn't certain what to think about it. Still, perhaps it was okay here. He recalled the films he had seen in the Ritz and Regal cinemas in Oxford, set in the depths of Africa; in these films, the natives had captured white missionaries and put them in a cooking pot, then danced around the pot, yelling war cries. If the Negroes could do something like that, well, perhaps then they deserved how they were being treated.

Meanwhile, they were trained to fly in a Boeing B-77 Flying Fortress under instruction for 60-65 hours. After six hours training the instructor said to Roger, "Okay, Bowler, off you go solo."

So he did. This was a tremendous thrill. It was just one circuit, but he sang and shouted because of being up in the air. He could fly!

Shortly after this, Roger learnt they were about to be sent to Arcadia, Florida where they were told there was a swimming pool and also that once there they would only sleep four to a room, which sounded good to him. But before this was to happen, he was taken ill with sharp pains in his stomach. He was sent to the De Soto Memorial Hospital where he was diagnosed with appendicitis. After an operation, he needed to convalesce at the hospital for a while and it during this convalescence that he made the acquaintance of eighteen-year- old, Belinda Jones who was a nurse-aid. She had just brought him his meals at first, but when the hospital put on a dance she'd told him about it. "It'll be great fun, hon'. Do you dance?"

"Certainly do."

"That's good. You will come, won't you?"

Roger didn't need a second invitation "Just try and keep me away."

Her face lit up. "Great, hon'!"

It was obvious that she was extremely attracted to him. He was attracted to her, partly, he imagined because of her soft Southern accent, so different to what he was used to. He'd danced every dance with her. As he got to know her better, he learnt that having no real nursing qualifications, a nurse-aid was the equivalent of an auxiliary nurse in England. Belinda was very different to Susan, not only in looks; her hair was light brown and not fair like Susan's, but in her nature; she was far less serious. She saw fun in everything. The serious nature of Susan could have been because she was an only child, whereas Belinda, who told him that her parents ran a farm near Gulf Shores, also had several brothers and sisters. She would tell him stories of how they used to go fishing from the pier at Gulf Shores and have competitions between themselves to see who could catch the most fish. Mostly, she added proudly, she had won the competition. The fish had been stored in their icebox until needed.

The idea of her liking fishing pleased Roger, it being his favourite hobby, though in his case it had been river fishing. So when she invited him to the farm for a few days to meet her folks, he'd accepted eagerly. He had told her when they'd first met that he was engaged to a girl back home, but she didn't seem too concerned about the fact. So he told himself that if she wasn't bothered about this, why should he be?

They travelled together by Greyhound bus to the farm. The farmhouse itself, like the majority of the other properties in Alabama was built of wood, as were the other smaller outbuildings nearby that he thought housed livestock. Parked nearby was a rackety old vehicle in which Roger imagined Belinda's father fetched any provisions the family might need from the nearby towns. The farmhouse and the outbuildings were surrounded by fields as far as the eye could see in which cows grazed. He heard the sound of snuffling and grunting. Looking in its direction he saw wide snouts and curly tails in a sty – pigs – a sow and several piglets – obviously being fattened with scraps from the family's table. His mouth watered. Roast pork and crackling. His favourite!

Her family were very welcoming, though there seemed to be so many of them, her parents and her brothers and sisters (she had two, Brenda and Betsy, both some years younger) all talking at once with similar accents to Belinda that he found difficult to get used to. He learnt he was to share a room with a couple of her brothers, Jimbo and Johnny, who were a similar age to Roger's own younger brother, Alec. All four of them were still at school, as unlike England, children didn't leave school at fourteen but went on until they were eighteen. Unlike, England, too, where most children went to schools within walking distance, here schools were mostly some distance away, and a bus came each morning to pick up Belinda's siblings. Pop Jones was sparse in build, with greying hair to match, while Mom Jones was plump and with faded fair hair. She fussed around pressing him to try this and that at meal times, though he didn't care for Grits as it reminded him of cold porridge. All the same, after the rationing back home, it was the plentiful food which impressed him the most, the bacon, pork, eggs, milk and cream. A seed of an idea began to grow within him that it would be a great life in America once the war was over, especially here down on the farm. Though of course a future in America was out of the question as he knew that Susan would never want to emigrate, leave her parents. And did he really want to leave his? Never see them or his two brothers again.

He and Belinda went fishing from the pier where they caught Amberjacks, Trigger fish and White snapper. Some Ma Jones cooked and some she put into an icebox to use later. An icebox was something he had never seen before. This wasn't the only thing that surprised him, they had a telephone too which no one he knew in England had in their homes as it was only middle-class and business people who could afford such things. While he was at the farm a special event occurred, a picnic was held at the pier. He and Belinda attended. As well as all the other unfamiliar food on offer there was Gumbo. This turned out to be a kind of stew which was made from okra, a vegetable that was new to him as well as a variety of fish. Belinda held out a small dish to him. He gingerly took a mouthful, chewed and swallowed.

"Well, what you think of it?" she queried with a smile.

Roger took another mouthful. "Mm. Quite tasty. I'll have another helping if I may?"

He did, and also a third helping.

Back at the farm he saw her doing something that he couldn't have imagined Susan would, or could do, in a million years. Mom Jones had wanted a chicken for the evening meal. This was to be one of their own chickens, one that had stopped laying eggs. Belinda had offered to see to the chicken. In disbelief, he watched her as she took the squawking chicken by its head and one of its legs and swung it deftly over her head to break its neck. Despite watching the bird's decease, it hadn't impaired his appetite when he came to eat it.

Meanwhile, the relationship between him and Belinda was developing. Wandering together along the deserted dirt track that led to the farm it had not taken long before they were enjoying passionate kisses and more. He didn't feel guilty about Susan back in England. He was engaged it was true, but so were many of the other chaps that he knew, some were even married with children but it didn't stop them having affairs if they got the chance.

He pulled Belinda to him. She responded as he knew she would. She was a hot cookie compared to Susan as she never pushed him away like Susan did when his hands began to wander, though he still hadn't experienced what he was dying to experience.

His lips pressed against hers and as he caressed her still clothed but willing body, excitement filled him.

She caressed him in return. Soon their discarded clothing lay in a pile beside them. "Are you sure?" he moaned.

"Yes, yes," she gasped...

The sexual act between them was all he had expected and more. They managed several more lovemaking sessions before it was time for them to return to the hospital. Soon afterwards, the doctors decided he was now fit enough to continue his pilot training, this time in Arcadia, Florida.

He'd not liked parting company with Belinda, his emotions were stirred up to such a fever pitch that he decided he must be in love with her. He'd certainly never felt like this with Susan. Belinda obviously had strong feeling for him too as awaiting the train at the railroad station and releasing her for a moment from his embrace he saw she was in tears. He gently wiped them away with his pocket handkerchief and kissed her trembling lips. "Don't worry, we can exchange letters."

"Letters are all very well, but when will I see you again, hon?"

"Soon, I'm sure to get some leave. We'll meet up then."

"But what if I find out that I'm pregnant?"

Before he could reply the train steamed in and he, along with all the other waiting passengers, surged towards it and climbed in. Doors banged, wheels rolled. Roger and Belinda waved frantically to each other for as long as they were able. Reluctantly, he seated himself. Feeling like he did about Belinda perhaps he ought to write to Susan and break off their engagement?

CHAPTER FIVE

Recognizing Roger's handwriting, Susan ripped open the envelope eagerly. It was time she'd had another letter from him, it had been weeks since she'd had the last one. She scanned the words that didn't seem to make sense to her, then reread them again more closely. She couldn't believe it? How could he do this to her? 'I'm sorry, Susan, but I feel I must break off our engagement as I've met an American girl. We're in love...'

In love! No! Her throat felt tight. She swallowed with difficulty. She had never looked at anyone else all the time she had known him, although she could have had several chances at Chapel if she'd encouraged the young men amongst the congregation. She'd not even gone with Angela to the dances at the Town Hall and the Carfax Assembly Rooms as she didn't want to risk meeting anyone and being tempted to go out with them, after all, only seeing Roger once in a while, she was lonely. And, now she may as well have gone to the dances. He was jilting her. How was she going to face her friends at the New Road Baptist Chapel? Everyone would feel so sorry for her. She decided to stop attending. She'd have to tell her parents about her broken engagement before they heard of this from Mr and Mrs Bowler. He would be sure to write and tell his parents of his decision. And who was this Yankee who had stolen her man? Perhaps though, once he had returned to England all this would die a natural death. After all, there would be thousands of miles between him and the Yankee. Would he then turn back to her, and would she still want him if he did?

Her mother was washing up in the kitchen.

"Mum," she said, swallowing with difficulty, "I've got something to tell you."

Her mother put the cup back into the dishwater. "What is it?"

Wordlessly, Susan held out Roger's letter."

Her mother scanned it. Her lips tightened. "I can't say I'm surprised, I never really trusted him. It was obvious he had a roving eye. Don't worry love, you'll find someone else ten times better than him."

"But I don't want anyone else," sniffed Susan, scrubbing at her cheek with her handkerchief.

Her mother placed an arm around her. "You say that now, but later on, you'll think differently. I know, I've been young once myself."

Eyeing her mother's tired-looking face, greying hair and sagging figure, she couldn't quite believe that!

"I won't, I won't! I love Roger, and only him." But the following day she rang Angela at the offices at Morris Motors, Cowley where she worked and made arrangements to go with her to the Saturday night dance at the Town Hall.

Saturday evening came. She examined herself in her mother's cheval mirror. She had put on her best dress. It was of blue cotton and matched her eyes. Before clothes rationing had begun she'd bought the material at the Cattle Market which was held every Wednesday at the Ox pens and made the dress herself on Mrs Bowler's sewing machine. After examining the reflection of the back of her legs to see if she'd drawn a straight line down them with an eyebrow pencil in lieu of stockings, she brushed her hair until it shone, and outlined her lips with a pale pink lipstick. She smiled with satisfaction. Yes, she'd do!

She called for Angela and the two girls' got the bus to Carfax.

In St Aldates, they climbed up the steep stone steps leading to the Town Hall where a dance was to be held that evening. Once inside, they bought tickets from the box office. Then, after depositing their coats in the cloakroom, they entered the crowded ballroom with its vaulted ceiling and ornate pillars where a lively number had just struck up and found two vacant seats at the edge of the floor. Seconds later she realised a tall and personable man was stood before her. "Can I have the pleasure?" he asked.

She stood up, giving him a friendly smile and taking his hand in her right hand, put her left hand on to his shoulder. They took to the floor. After the usual, "Do you come here often?" followed by the two of them exchanging names – his was Sam Walker, he confided that he was a fireman and exempt from being called up because of the nature of his work.

They had several dances together after this, dances she enjoyed; he was light on his feet and a better dancer even than Roger. Before the last dance had ended he had asked if he could take her home. She'd agreed, he seemed very nice and by the way he was looking at her there was a good chance before they got to her front door he would be asking if they could see each other again? Well, that would be all right by her, she couldn't stay a nun for the rest of her life just because Roger didn't want her. She supposed too that being a fireman wasn't as dangerous as being an airman. At least, she hoped not!

Retrieving her coat from the attendant in the cloakroom she had a word with Angela who was also about to get her coat. She told her about Sam and how he had offered to see her home. "You don't mind, do you?"

"Of course not. Besides," she added with a twinkle in her eyes, "I've got an escort for the walk home too."

CHAPTER SIX

Belinda studied Roger's latest letter. He didn't say whether he had finished with the English girl as he'd promised to do – so maybe he hadn't. Disappointed, she swallowed the lump in her throat. Roger was due to go back to England soon as the American Air Force had decided he wasn't fit enough to become a pilot – his lack of fitness was something she imagined was due to when he had had his appendicitis operation, though she couldn't be certain if this was correct.

If he should leave without making things official with her, she could lose him – three thousand miles was an almost unimaginable distance. It could be a case of out of sight, out of mind. He'd probably just continue with his engagement to that Susan - especially if he hadn't actually broken it off with her. She couldn't bear that to happen. She was so much in love, fascinated, she supposed by his English accent. She had had a few other boyfriends in the past but she'd never felt about them as she did about Roger. What she needed to do was to get him to marry her before he left for the UK – perhaps she could write and tell him that she was worried that she might be pregnant? He might offer to make her Mrs Bowler if he imagined that. She could always tell him afterwards that she must have made a mistake as regards a baby. She squashed down any guilty feelings about telling him a lie. He was coming again soon to visit her at the farm when she had leave from the hospital, so it would only be a matter of time before there actually was a baby, if their mad passionate lovemaking was anything to go by.

Satisfied, she picked up her fountain pen and replied to what he had written. Roger's answer was all that she had desired – she was to make arrangements for their wedding immediately. This she did. She wrote to her parents to tell them the exciting news. The letter she had in return showed that her mother had mixed feelings about her marrying Roger; although Belinda had several other siblings, she wasn't keen on her possibly ending up living in England, so very far away. All the same, the arrangements were soon made for them to be married in April 1942. The ceremony was to be held at the house as was usual in Alabama and performed by a Justice of the Peace. Her mother promised to make a cake and invitations were to be sent out to all their family and friends, amongst the guests' would be her favourite uncle, Uncle Stan, her mother's brother, who was one of the two senators for Alabama. Unassuming as regards appearance; slightly built with wispy grey hair, he had a forceful personality which no doubt had got him to where he was today. She decided to write to him.

Knowing she needed a special dress to get married in she went to a dress shop to buy a suitable dress. After trying on several, she decided on a pale pink ankle length silk dress. Then having arranged some extra leave from the hospital, she went home. The day before the wedding, Roger arrived, accompanied by Charlie, one of his mates, who was to be Roger's best man.

Arm-in-arm, walking to their favourite secluded spot for lovemaking – having got one of her girl friends' to take care of Charlie, she whispered. "When you go home, Roger, we won't be apart for long as Uncle Stan will pull strings to get me to England."

"Can he do that?"

She smiled. America had entered the war on the 7th of December 1941 and American troops were now being sent to England. "I think so, especially as I'm a nurse-aid. He'll let the authorities think I'm a qualified nurse. With being in an influential position, it won't be difficult for him to get permission for me to sail to the U.K. to nurse our boys." What an adventure it would be to actually go to England. None of her friends had ever travelled abroad. When she got there would Roger take her to London? Would she see Buckingham Palace and the King and Queen of England? What a thrill that would be! She wondered what Roger's family, especially his mother would think of her – a foreigner? Probably they would rather he had married his long-time girlfriend, whom, according to Roger, they knew well. Mr and Mrs Bowler were even close friends with Susan's parents. Would the split between their daughter and Roger spoil the friendship between the older couples? Oh, well, she couldn't help that. And they would just have to get used to her – it wasn't up to them – it was up to Roger whom he chose as his wife.

He hugged her to him. "That's wonderful."

They sank to the ground and as usual nature took its course.

* * *

It was early evening. On the arm of her father, Pop Jones, Belinda entered the room that was filled with flowers to loud applause from family and friends. She saw Roger waiting for her. Moving towards him, she took his hand. He squeezed hers encouragingly. Then standing in front of the smiling Justice of the Peace, they made their vows to each other. She felt like a princess in her pink dress, she imagined that none of the girls in England would have such a stylish wedding dress with there now being clothes rationing over there. After a slap-up wedding breakfast which Roger told her contained food items that they rarely were able to obtain in England, she shyly said her 'good nights' to everyone; went to her room and put on the pretty white nightdress with embroidered flowers around the neckline that she had also bought for the occasion from the dress shop. Picking up the bottle of Chantilly from her dressing table, a popular fragrance by Dana which had just come onto the market, containing, according to the label on the bottle, bergamot, lemon, spices, carnation, jasmine and musk; she pulled out the glass stopper and sniffed with pleasure. She dabbed the perfume generously onto her forehead, behind her ears and wrists, also onto the neck of her nightgown and even some of the sheet. That should get him going. She thrilled at the thoughts milling through her head. Not that he usually needed much getting going.

She climbed into bed.

She waited and waited. She eyed her bedside clock – it was almost midnight – she had heard the guests' cars revving up and leaving ages ago. Surely, too, all the family must have retired for the night by now? She couldn't understand it; surely he would be as keen to get her into their marriage bed as she was to get him. A mixture of anger and disappointment filled her.

The door opened. "Sorry, sweetheart," he mumbled, "but I couldn't get away from your Uncle Stan, he does go on and on. He wanted to know all about life in England and the RAF – evidently he'd always wanted to fly. When I eventually managed to get away I didn't know which bedroom was yours. In fact, I barged into the wrong room and woke your parents, who didn't seem pleased."

Belinda relieved, laughed, and patted the place beside her. "You're here now – come on, let's make up for lost time."

Roger needed no second invitation. He stripped off his clothing, threw everything over a chair, and then climbed in beside her. He pulled her to him and caressed her more than willing body. She giggled at his eagerness. Soon the bedsprings were complaining of what was taking place upon them.

* * *

She had packed her suitcases with her new clothes she had bought especially for her trip to England. She picked up the framed photograph of her and Roger taken on their wedding day. Before placing it in one of her suitcases she kissed the image of Roger. This photo was one of her most prized possession. It would always have pride of place in any house she lived in. Her passport had been acquired with the help of her Uncle Stan, and she was to leave the following morning on the first leg of her journey to the U.K. Roger had already left the US of A, a fortnight earlier. She'd received a letter from him to say he had arrived back safely and had returned to his RAF base.

She looked around her room. Would she ever see it again – was it really so dangerous to trust herself to the high seas? Well, she had to, despite her mother's warnings of submarines and ending up as fish food – that's if the ship she was on wasn't blasted to smithereens by torpedoes, she just had to join her husband – she couldn't wait until the war was over. She felt hot all over thinking of the lovemaking in this very room. She needed to enjoy it again and soon, and perhaps, this time she'd find herself pregnant. Lain in her bed, too excited and apprehensive to drop off, she tossed and turned for hours and was grateful when she heard her mother getting up to prepare breakfast. At this, she rose and put on one of her new outfits.

"There you are," said Mom, "get this inside you."

She pecked at her mother's biscuits and scrambled egg, and at last gave it up as a bad job.

A few hours later; kisses and hugs behind her, she was on the Greyhound bus to Montgomery where she changed trains for St Johns, Newfoundland. At St Johns she embarked on 'The Denver' bound for Liverpool.

She was directed to her cabin. There was a porthole at one end and eight bunks, one on top of the other. This cabin she soon realised was to be shared with several other young women, nurses on their way to nurse their American boys in England.

"Do you want a top bunk or a lower bunk?" asked a blue-eyed bubbly blonde.

"What do you fancy, hon?"

"I don't mind. By the way my name's Gillian, Gillian Adams. What's your name?"

"Belinda, Belinda Bowler."

"Hi. Belinda."

"Hi. Gillian."

They settled on a top bunk for Gillian and a lower one

for herself. The other girls sharing the cabin were called, Jane, Jean, Angela, Louise, Brenda and Peggy (short for Margaret). Belinda was the only one who was married, and when she showed them a photo of Roger in his RAF uniform, they were all envious. "He's a dish, you are lucky."

The girls went up on deck and watched as the dockside slid past. They heard a siren and felt a shudder beneath their feet. They were on their way. Belinda felt apprehensive, what if she was a bad sailor and got seasick? She found the truth of this a few days later when there was a mighty storm and everyone was so affected by the mountainous seas that they had to lay on their bunks holding brown paper sick bags beneath their chins.

At last, the North Sea quietened. She had made friends with the other girls and as day followed day she learnt all their past history. Apart from nursing their poor boys in the UK they all hoped to meet up with a rich Limey, a lord or a duke with a country estate where they could end up as Lady of the Manor. She smiled at that, she knew that Roger, despite being an officer, only came from a working class family that lived in a terraced house. She had had a letter from her new father-in-law telling her this. He'd not wanted her getting inflated ideas about his son's family; he knew how Roger liked to pretend he was more than he actually was.

She strolled along the deck, before settling in a deckchair with a magazine. Only a couple of days to go now, she thought before we reach Liverpool, but fate was to prove differently. That night she woke abruptly at hearing a tremendous bang and feeling the ship shudder. "What is that? What's happened?"

Immediately a siren sounded and across the intercom a voice said, "Abandon ship! Abandon ship!"

"Abandon ship!" she screeched, as the truth struck her. Despite being in the midst of a convoy of ships which was supposed to be protecting 'The Denver', they had been torpedoed. "Oh, God, we're all going to die!" She hurriedly climbed out of her bunk.

The other girls, yawning widely climbed out of their bunks and reached for their daytime clothing.

"No time for that, we've got to get up on deck immediately. Get your life jackets on!"

Everyone struggled into them, then clad in night clothes and slippers, and only pausing to pick up their handbags containing their papers, they left the cabin.

As they reached the deck more deafening explosions sounded beneath them, followed by bright orange flames which poured from the companionways. Everyone was coughing, black smoke, thicker than a forest fire, choking them. A screaming figure covered with flames appeared from the fiery hell that was raging in the belly of the ship, whether male or female she couldn't tell. To her horror, in desperation, it threw itself over the ship's rails and into the sea. On deck, dozens of people, some praying, some cursing, "Bloody Germans!" were milling around in a panic as lifeboats were hastily lowered. One crowded lifeboat began to descend; as it did so it capsized, tipping its hysterical cargo into the choppy sea. Some of her companions climbed into another boat - there wasn't room for her, much to her distress; she would have rather kept with her new friends. Fortunately, the one containing her friends made it down safely.

Belinda climbed into another lifeboat, praying to herself that this one wouldn't capsize like the first one had. Her prayer must have been answered as it didn't. Four sailors were at the oars and they rowed as quickly as they could away from the sinking ship. She saw some drifting wreckage with people clinging to it. On something that looked to her like a wooden shelf, a young man was crying, "Mum! Mum!" Then he slid from the wreckage, and with a gurgle, disappeared as the waves closed over him.

Some swimmers approached their lifeboat, to her distress she saw the sailors' beat them away with the oars. She realised that they really had no choice, that their boat couldn't take any more people without it sinking, it was already overloaded. Frozen in horror, she watched the bow of 'The Denver' rise up; then silently slip into the depths of the moonlit ocean.

How long they were in the lifeboat she had no idea – it seemed like forever. Her stomach hurt, it was so empty – a few ships' biscuits that had been stored in the boat beneath the seats in case of emergencies and a few sips of water couldn't fill it. At least though, with not much to drink they didn't need to relieve themselves that often over an empty ships' biscuits container. When they needed to leave their seats they had to be very careful how they moved.

Along with the ships' biscuits stored beneath the seats were some blankets and a tarpaulin. This tarpaulin was used to fix up a shelter for them to take turns to rest beneath the blankets.

One of the nurses who was seated beside her died and after a hasty prayer said by one of the sailors; she was tipped over the side.

In a dreamlike state, to her astonishment, she felt a hand pulling at the buttons of her pyjama jacket. The hand belonged to a ships' steward, a man in his fifties who had taken the empty seat beside her. He leered and his flabby lips pressed on hers as his other hand slipped inside the waist of her pyjama trousers. She struggled, horrified, "Get off! Leave me alone!"

To her relief, he was pulled off her. Her rescuer, a young US soldier, landed a blow on her attacker's chin. He fell backwards and over the side of the lifeboat. He thrashed about in the water. "Help! I can't swim."

Someone threw the man a lifebelt, but it fell some distance from him – too far away for him to reach. Seeing this, not thinking of the danger to himself, the soldier leapt over the side of the lifeboat and caught hold of the back of the man's shirt, just as, with a gurgling sound, he sank down beneath the waves for the third time.

The soldier pulled him upwards. With effort, he swam back to the lifeboat. He pulled the man back over the side.

He lay there, in the bottom of the boat like an inert jellyfish.

She refastened her pyjama jacket. "Thank you, oh, thank you."

"Don't mention it, only too pleased to be of help." He sank back onto a bench, ignoring the wet clothing that clung to him.

Some days later, when the fresh water was almost exhausted, it began to rain. At this, everyone lifted their heads back and opened their mouths to drink the life giving rainwater, which also filled the barrel in which the drinking water was stored. But now, with the rain becoming torrential rain, water was swishing around at the bottom of the boat, and everyone had to take the empty ships' biscuit containers and use them as balers.

It was sometime after this that someone suddenly exclaimed. "Ship ahoy!"

Belinda looked in the direction of the pointing finger. It was indeed a ship though still a long way off.

The ship came nearer. It was a British ship called the RMS Lloyd George.

It came alongside and one of the crew threw down a rope ladder.

She carefully climbed up the swaying ladder and onto the ship where a blanket was placed around her shivering shoulders, and she was given a hot drink. She learnt from the British sailor that the RMS Lloyd George was en route from Bombay, India, to Tilbury Docks. She also learnt that 'The Denver' had been torpedoed in the North Sea and their lifeboat had then drifted into the English Channel. As she sipped her tea she noticed with some satisfaction that the man who had attempted to maul her, now wearing handcuffs, was being hustled by two burly sailors down to the bowels of the ship.

Having recovered somewhat, she was taken below decks herself to a cabin where exhausted she sank thankfully on to a bunk and soon fell asleep. Later, after eating a meal which she was told to chew slowly and swallow carefully, she was examined by the ship's doctor who decided she was fit enough to disembark when they reached Tilbury and go on her way. "You were lucky you weren't in that lifeboat for very long."

"Ten days seemed a long time to me."

"I suppose it would, but there have been people who have had to spend three weeks in a lifeboat and needed hospital treatment afterwards."

"How awful! I'm glad is wasn't that long before we were picked up." She wriggled uncomfortably. "But even if I can now go on my way, how can I travel anywhere clad in damp pyjamas and dressing gown?" she said.

The doctor looked thoughtful. "Don't worry my dear, there's several ladies travelling on this ship. Perhaps I can get someone to be a Good Samaritan and spare you a few items of clothing. "

"I'll need shoes, too."

"What size do you take?"

She told him.

Shortly afterwards he returned with a pair of sturdy brown brogues, a ladies' tweed costume and a short woollen jacket. Belinda thanked him profusely, but as she put on the shoes and dressed herself in the costume and jacket; which were only slightly too large for her, she thought with regret of all her lovely new clothing that was now at the bottom of the ocean. She had imagined she would be the envy of all the English girls when she was dressed in these outfits, especially as new clothing was in short supply as far as they were concerned.

At last, tugs manoeuvred the ship into the dock.

As she descended the gangplank she saw the young soldier that had saved her from being mauled. He turned and recognized her. "Are you all right now, hon?"

"Yes, and thanks for everything."

"That's okay. By the way my name is Hank, Hank Watson."

"Mine's Belinda, Belinda Bowler."

"So where are you heading for Belinda?"

"Oxford. My husband's folks live there."

He looked disappointed. "Oh!"

By his expression, she guessed he had hoped she was single. "So where are you heading, Hank?"

"Didcot."

She had never heard the name before so had no idea that the US Army camp was near to Oxford.

CHAPTER SEVEN

Agatha Bowler took the telegram from the telegraph boy's hand – her own was shaking. Was it bad news? Had her Roger been killed, his aircraft shot down by those German swine's. If this had happened she'd be devastated. She thought of a woman whom she'd known slightly who used to live in West Street. She'd met her when they were both queuing up at the butchers in the Botley Road for off the ration sausages on one occasion, and another, for whale meat. Her boy, also air crew like her Roger, and an only child had been killed in a raid over Germany. A widow, she'd never got over her loss and eventually she'd ended up being taken away by the yellow van to Littlemore Mental Asylum.

The words danced before her eyes:

'Arriving midday STOP Looking forward
to seeing everyone STOP
Love STOP. Belinda. XXX '

Agatha swallowed. Belinda! So the Yankee was on her way. She'd hoped with the war raging she would never actually get here. She'd wanted Roger to marry Susan. She felt sure that Susan would have been the daughter she'd never had. Now, according to her friend, Mavis Swift, Susan was courting someone else, a fireman. It was a real shame that Roger had been sent to America. And even more of a shame that he had met this Belinda. She was certain that the girl wouldn't settle here in this country, she was probably used to a more exotic lifestyle, mixing with film stars and the like. She herself had had a job settling in Oxford when she'd first come here, and she wasn't a foreigner like her. She'd certainly not liked Oxford at all. On her way to the Town and the Covered Market off the High Street where she did most of her shopping; the small shops that she passed in Hythe Bridge Street were so shabby and certainly not much an advertisement for a University city. The canal, too, which ran alongside Hythe Bridge Street and was green with algae stunk.

She had met George, Roger's father in 1916. This had occurred in Wales, where, at that time she was in Service. Having been born in Box, near Bath, she had previously been in Service in Bath from the age of twelve. She had come to Wales to be near her elder brother, Bert, who worked on the railway in Pontypool.

On that day she had been hanging out the washing for the Mistress in the back garden and the railway line ran alongside the bottom of it. A train, surrounded by clouds of smoke steamed past. She saw two men on the footplate. Despite their blackened faces she recognised the train driver, the elder of the two, he attended the Baptist chapel where she worshipped on Sundays. She had waved to them and they had waved back to her.

The following Sunday, Mr Green introduced her to George who was the fireman, stoking the engine. Despite only seeing each other on Sunday afternoons, and her one half day off once a fortnight, love had blossomed and a couple of months later, when George, who had only been temporary on the Welsh railway, was transferred back to his home town, Oxford, she gave in her notice and went there herself where she had lodged with George's family. George was one of eight, six boys and two girls and she'd needed to share a double bed in their front room with his sisters, until in 1918, they had found a terraced house to rent in Osney and were able to be married.

She put the telegram on the mantelpiece and wondered what George would say when he came in from work?

He never had much to say on the subject when he came in, but Roger's younger brother, Alec certainly did. Glaring, he said, "Why is she coming here, Mum? Perhaps if she stayed in her own country Roger might get back with Susan."

Agatha sighed. She knew that Alec was upset that Susan no longer visited them. She had always taken a lot of notice of him, playing cards and shove ha'penny and probably letting Alec win more often than not. In her opinion Susan would have suited Alec more than she did Roger, though of course, Alec was rather young for her.

"Look, Alec. You've got to be grown-up about this. That could never happen. This Belinda and our Roger are married, and once you are married, you have made your choice of husband or wife and that is that! There is no going back."

"Couldn't they get a divorce?"

"No, they couldn't, we're a respectable family. Besides something like that would cost a lot of money. Far more than we could ever afford!"

"Well, don't expect me to welcome her!" Alec turned and stamped out of the room.

* * *

Arriving at Oxford Station, Belinda took a taxi to Bridge Street, Osney. She had no idea how far away Roger's home was, it might have been miles from the station for all she knew. In the end, it wasn't such a great distance, in fact she could have easily walked it. They drove over the bridge for which the street was named. The taxi drew up outside the terraced house which was in a street of terraced houses, the front doors of which all opened straight onto the sidewalk. "This is it," said the driver.

"How much?" she asked.

"One shilling," he replied.

She fumbled in her bag to locate her purse. Was a shilling a lot of money or not? And which coin amongst so many unfamiliar coins, was it? She'd no idea, and hoping that the taxi driver was honest, she offered him her open purse. "Help yourself," she said.

He located a silver coin and took it out. He held it up to show her, "That's a shilling," he explained. He held up a nickel coin pointedly, "and that's a penny. Twelve of them make a shilling."

Thanking him, giving him the shilling as well as the penny as a tip she alighted and trembling slightly as much from coolness of the climate as from apprehension, knocked at the door with the heavy metal knocker shaped like a fish.

She heard footsteps and seconds later the door opened, revealing a short middle- aged woman who was as round as a ball with greying hair that was fastened in a bun behind her head. "Yes?" she said.

"Mrs Bowler?"

"Yes, I'm Mrs Bowler."

"I'm Belinda, Roger's wife. You got my telegram, didn't you?"

A shadow passed across the older woman's face. "Yes, you'd best come in. Haven't you any luggage?"

She explained about being torpedoed and losing everything. "I've only got what I'm standing up in." Her throat thickened and she swallowed hard as she recalled the awful events that she was certain she would never forget.

"I see. We'll have to get you a change of clothing at least." Her mother-in-law turned and headed off back down the passage, saying over her shoulder. "They'll have to be second-hand I'm afraid as you won't have any clothing coupons. Not until you register for your ration book. Even when you have clothing coupons new clothes aren't exactly easy to get your hands on. For most people it's a case of make- do-and-mend."

Belinda followed Mrs Bowler along the narrow passage and into which she imagined was the living room. She stood there awkwardly.

"You'd best sit down. I'll make you a cup of tea."

She sat gingerly on the edge of a hard-backed chair. "Thanks, but could I have coffee?"

Her mother-in-law lifted the huge black kettle from the hob over the fire in the black-leaded range and poured hot water into the brown earthenware teapot on the table, after which she placed a red knitted tea cosy over the pot. She took two cups and saucers from the tall wall cupboard. "Not got any. I used to get Camp coffee in a bottle before the war, but like most things nowadays it's difficult to get hold of."

Belinda sipped at the sugarless tea, she guessed that sugar was on ration too. How she wished Roger was with her. At least then, the strangeness of everything wouldn't be quite so hard to bear. She noticed a framed copy of her wedding photograph on the mantelpiece and recalled that she and Roger had sent it to England for his parents. Tears filled her eyes as the realisation hit her that her wedding photo that she had been so proud of was now with all her other belongings at the bottom of the ocean.

"What's wrong?" asked Mrs Bowler.

Belinda explained.

She looked thoughtful, then seemingly made up her mind. She indicated the photograph on the mantelpiece. "You'd best have this one."

"Are you sure?"

"I certainly am. "She handed it to her.

"That's very good of you. I'm very grateful."

After a midday meal, a stew made by the boiling up ham bones with the addition of some vegetables from Mr Bowler's allotment - this meal Mr Bowler shared with them – the Railway Workshops where he was employed being only a five minute walk away, Mrs Bowler showed her to her bedroom. It was very small and hardly had room for a double bed and a wardrobe. Under the bed was a white china chamber pot. This, she gathered was to be used at night –as there was only an outside toilet in the backyard.

She seated herself on the edge of the bed which was covered by a patchwork quilt. She decided to write to Roger to tell him she had arrived in Oxford. She hoped it wouldn't be long before he got some leave. She couldn't wait to see him again and enjoy what they had both enjoyed in America.

Later that day, Roger's young brother, Alec, returned

from work. Now fourteen, and a younger version of Roger, he had recently left school and was working at the Electric Light Works. Mrs Bowler introduced him to her, but she could tell from his mumbled, "Hello" that she would get no welcome from him. It didn't help her case, she supposed that she had no present to bring him from America, the gifts she had brought for Roger's family having ended up where all her other belongings were. At the bottom of the ocean.

That night her sleep was disturbed by dreams, or rather nightmares of her time in the lifeboat – choking from the black smoke, seeing and feeling the heat of flames, hearing cries and seeing bloated bodies floating in the sea. She awoke with a start knowing she had called out and hoping she'd not disturbed the rest of the household.

The next morning, after a meagre breakfast, consisting of a couple slices of toast thinly spread with margarine and more sugarless tea, she walked up to Walton Street and the Radcliffe Infirmary, having been shown the way there for a few coppers by Bob Paxton, a young boy who lived next door. She'd hoped to get a job at the hospital as a nurse. This never came about as she had no real nursing qualifications. She was offered a job as a cleaner, but declined, she felt she was too good for such mundane work. Despondently, after registering with the Ministry of Food for a ration book, and getting a few items of clothing from a second-hand shop she returned to her in law's house.

She picked at the midday meal, which according to her mother-in-law was Woolton pie, one of Lord Woolton's recipes – diced potatoes, cauliflower, swedes, carrots, onions and oatmeal, which was covered in pastry and baked. She pushed her plate aside. She'd no real appetite. Besides, it seemed rather bland after the food she was used to.

What could she do now? She needed a job so she could give the Bowlers' some money each week for her keep.

As if reading her thoughts, Mrs Bowler said, "Why

don't you try the Serviceman's Club in Cornmarket in the centre of Town? You will have passed it on your way to the hospital. "

"I think I know where you mean."

"Good! It used to be the Clarendon Hotel. Very swish it was, all the nobs stayed there. They might take you on."

Mr Bowler chewed and swallowed a mouthful of his mock apricot tart and custard - grated sweetened carrots in a pastry case. "That's a good idea," he agreed.

Belinda frowned. "Swish, and nobs, she had no idea what her mother-in-law was on about. The English these English spoke was very peculiar. "Do you think so?"

"It's worth a try, isn't it?"

She decided her mother-in-law was right and she decided to go there and try her luck that very afternoon.

It was a huge four-storey building, and some of her countrymen calling to one another were hanging out of the upper windows. She opened the door and went in. A jukebox in the corner of the room was playing a popular tune. There was a dart board on the wall, and nearby, a couple of pool tables. Several American servicemen were seated at the small tables, chatting, smoking and drinking coffee. At one side of the room, a middle- aged woman also in uniform and with rather brassy hair piled on top of her head was seated behind a desk. She approached her. "Excuse me, ma'am," she said.

The woman looked up. "What can I do for you?" she asked in a strong Southern accent.

"I'm looking for work, ma'am, have you any vacancies? I'm willing to do anything. "

The woman looked surprised at hearing a similar accent to her own. "You're American, aren't you? What are you doing in the U.K?"

"I'm married to an English airman," explained Belinda. We met in Alabama. He was training as a pilot. He's back now at his camp in Lincolnshire. I sailed from the U.S. of A. a couple of weeks ago to be with him. My husband's family live in Oxford so that is why I am here."

"Hmm, well, if you are interested I could offer you a job as a waitress."

"Could you ma'am? That'd be wonderful."

"So could you start immediately?"

"Certainly could, ma'am."

"So what's your name?"

"Belinda Bowler."

"Well, Belinda, take your coat off and hang it in the cloakroom, then start clearing the tables and washing up."

Several hours later, on her way back to Osney and her in laws, she felt like dancing. She'd got a job! She wouldn't be getting a big wage but at least she would be able to pay her way. When she got in, she found a letter for her on the mantelpiece. To her delight she recognised the handwriting. It was from Roger. Gleefully, she ripped it open and read what it said. That night she slept with it beneath her pillow. In it, Roger had said that he had a ten days leave starting a week Friday and would be coming home to Oxford. Now she had a job she wouldn't be able to spend much time during the day with him, but at least they would have the nights. Nights, she knew that would be full of passion!

With working from 10am to 6pm at the Servicemen's' Club, the days passed quicker than she'd expected. She was beginning to get used to living on Osney Island as everyone called the area, the river ran all the way around it, and there was South Street, East Street, West Street and North Street, with Bridge Street in the Centre. Her father-in-law who was quite a reader told her all about the history of the place. "In the Middle Ages," he explained, "this area was dominated by the Augustine Osney Abbey, which was founded in 1129 by Robert D'Oyley, one of William the Conqueror's men."

Belinda, who mostly read women's' magazines had no idea of this. "Really?"

"Yes, evidently Osney is shaped like an old fashioned belt buckle, with the streets named after the points of the compass. Osney Island features in Geoffrey Chaucer's,

'Canterbury Tales' – the 'Miller's Tale', and was developed for housing in 1851. By the mid 1850's most of the small terraces had been built, with the majority of the inhabitants being railway workers, like myself and Fred Paxton, the man next door to us."

All the same, despite having learnt the history of the area of Oxford where she was now living everything still seemed so strange to her. Here, they had different words for everything which caused her some confusion until she got used to them. The sidewalk was called the pavement, an elevator, a lift, the faucet, of which there was only one, and the water cold, was over the kitchen sink, and called a tap, the railroad, the railway. Then there was the rationing. The allowance of bacon and ham was only 2ozs a week per adult, butter also was 2ozs, cheese, 2ozs, margarine was 4ozs, sugar 8ozs, and eggs, 1 a week, though milk was two pints per person per week. As Mrs Bowler kept chickens, their squawking woke her up early each morning, they were able to enjoy an extra egg occasionally. Though not this week as Mrs Bowler was saving them to make Roger his favourite cake when he came home.

At last, she heard a taxi draw up outside, and then he was in the passage and she was in his arms. That night, and every night, was a night of passion – even banishing the nightmares she had been suffering from. Releasing herself from Roger's embrace she thought, surely I must be pregnant by now? The following morning before she left the house he suddenly said, "Would you like to go dancing while I'm here?"

"Dancing! I certainly would, though I've no idea what I'm going to wear." She thought regretfully of the pretty evening dresses she had bought before leaving the States.

She mentioned her problem to Olivia, the woman in charge at the Servicemen's club.

Olivia looked thoughtful. "Don't worry, hon, you can borrow one of mine. It's blue taffeta and has a full skirt, when he twirls you in a waltz it will swirl around you. It should fit you as we are much the same size. I'll bring it with me when I come in tomorrow and you can try it on. "

"That's really good of you. Thanks."

"Don't mention it, hon."

* * *

True to her word Olivia brought the dress in the next day. It was a perfect fit. She had also lent her some matching blue high heeled shoes, which also fortunately fitted. The dance was on the Saturday evening, and Belinda felt like a film star when she put the dress and shoes on. Olivia had also lent her a small fur jacket though although it was July, it could be rather chilly. They were going to a dance at the Town Hall, and Roger insisted they should have a taxi there. They arrived and climbed the steep stone steps to the entrance hall. She deposited the jacket in the cloakroom and eyed herself in the mirror with satisfaction. As she joined Roger in the crowded ballroom she wondered if Susan and her new boyfriend - the fireman, might take it into their heads to go dancing here tonight too. Though she had been with Roger to the New Road Baptist Chapel and Susan hadn't come there. Perhaps she was keeping away from the chapel on purpose not wanting to risk seeing her former fiancé with someone else. If she and Roger did run into them, it could be rather embarrassing, especially for that Susan. Still, why should she care? They seated themselves on the chairs at the edge of the floor. The band struck up a familiar number and she tapped her feet in time to the music. She expected him to say, "Come on, let's dance." To her astonishment though, he suddenly excused himself and going up to another girl, asked her to dance instead. Bemused, she sat there, until a young man came up and said, "Can I have the pleasure?"

Why not? she thought, if Roger can dance with another girl, surely I can dance with another man! She and the man had only danced a few steps together when Roger, having left his partner in the middle of the floor, cut in.

Determinedly, he took her back to her seat, then turning, went off and asked another girl to dance. What a cheek! she thought, and his behaviour quite spoilt her evening.

* * *

A few days later, Roger's leave being over, Belinda returned from the station after seeing him off. Seated on the bed she recalled his behaviour at the dance. She stared, red-eyed through the murky glass of their bedroom window. Where were these dreaming spires of Oxford she'd heard so much about? She couldn't see them! She decided she had a lot to learn about her husband. Could he be a philanderer? If so, why had he married her? She was no 'Betty Grable.' Apart from the mousy hair she put into bobby pins each night, all she had to commend her was that she was slim. A picture of Roger's eyes when had first seen their farm flashed before her as well as the details of the plans he'd made for life after the war. Her view of wet slates and dripping guttering momentarily changed to her pop's sunlit acres – stabbing her with something new and unexpected. Could he have wed her just so he could get his feet under their farmhouse table?

CHAPTER EIGHT

One day at the Servicemen's Club, Belinda was serving coffees to a group of Americans. She still wasn't pregnant much to her disappointment. Was it her fault or was it Roger's? Something was wrong that much was certain. Perhaps she should see a doctor?

She took the cups from a tray and placed them before them.

"Thanks, hon," they mutually exclaimed.

To her astonishment, one of them suddenly remarked, "I know you, don't I?"

She looked closer at the speaker. She decided he did seem rather familiar. Where had she seen him before? At last it came to her, it was the young soldier from the lifeboat who had come to her rescue. What a coincidence that they should meet up again here. Now what was his name? She thought for a moment or two. Hank; that was it!

"So how are you keeping Belinda?"

"You remember my name?"

"Yes, why not?"

She had no answer to that, after all she did remember his. She and Hank chatted for a few moments then she had to get on with her work. After that they saw each other on several occasions. He told her he came in quite often from his camp in Didcot, which she now discovered wasn't so far from Oxford. She found she was beginning to look forward to seeing him. It was good to meet up with a fellow countryman. To talk about things that the people here had no idea about. She did wonder if he was visiting the Servicemen's Club more than he had before, and that the reason might be herself. She supposed she shouldn't encourage him with her being a married woman. Oh, well, she didn't really care. She was lonely with Roger miles away and she didn't feel all that comfortable with her in laws either. To try to fool herself that this friendship was all above board she invited him to the Bowlers' house to meet them. Not only that, Hank was due to leave England shortly. The rumour going around his camp was that they were being sent to North Africa to fight in the desert with Montgomery against Rommel. A strange pang hit her at the thought of Hank going away and having to fight. Maybe even be killed. Was she becoming fonder of him than she realised? No, she thought, she loved Roger. And only Roger. Hank was no more than a friend.

So Hank came one evening bringing presents of tinned fruit and Lucky Strike cigarettes for Mr Bowler. Mr & Mrs Bowler seemed to like him, was interested to hear his tales of life in the U.S., but not so young Alec, she noticed him glaring at Hank when he thought that Hank wasn't looking. And when a game of cards was suggested, the Bowlers' were both keen card players, he refused to join in. Apart from Alec's moodiness the evening went off well.

A few days later, she decided to visit the doctor. She had been taken on by the Bowler's doctor, Doctor Green whose surgery was in the Botley Road. He was a pleasant middle-aged man with greying hair and a wispy beard, and someone to whom she felt she could confide such an intimate problem.

She entered his examination room. On one wall hung a skeleton, squeamishly she averted her eyes wondering if it might be a real one? There was also a couch where she imagined he did his examination of patients. Seated at his desk, writing something, he looked up. "Take a seat, Mrs Bowler," he said. What can I do for you?"

Blushing slightly, she explained.

"How long have you been trying for a baby?"

"About ten months, on and off," she said. "We're not always together, it's only when he comes on leave, Roger's in the RAF, Bomber Command, and stationed in Lincolnshire. He is a navigator on the Lancaster's," she added proudly.

"One of our brave boys. I see." He steepled his two index fingers, "Don't worry, my dear. Ten months isn't that long. With a first baby it could take as long as two years to become pregnant."

"Could it really?"

"Yes, but if you are worried, I could arrange for you to have some tests at the Gynaecological Department at the Radcliffe. If they find nothing wrong with you, which I'm sure will be the case, perhaps your husband should be tested too. It could be his fault."

"Could it? I don't think he'd be pleased to find that out."

He nodded. "Most men aren't."

She frowned. She'd heard the older women talking about men in general and knew that the majority would rather blame their wives for their lack of children, insist the wife must be barren. She supposed it made them feel less of a man if they couldn't get a woman pregnant. They certainly wouldn't want to admit to such a thing, even to themselves.

He rose from his seat and she did too.

He put out his hand to shake hers. "I'll be in touch when I have arranged an appointment for you at the hospital. "

"Thanks, Doctor Green."

She left his surgery and walked the short distance to Osney and the Bowler's house. She hoped that if there was something actually wrong with her the hospital could put it right. If it should turn out that it wasn't her that was at fault then she would have to tackle Roger about this sensitive subject. What his reaction would be she couldn't possibly imagine. The weeks passed, in which she saw Hank from time to time, walks along the tow-path of the river Thames, or trips to the cinema; their friendship was quite innocent, though she guessed, men being like they were, he might have liked it to be otherwise.

Doctor Green had arranged an examination for her at the Radcliffe Infirmary. Nervously, she found her way along corridors that smelt strongly of carbolic to the Gynaecology Department and approached a nurse in black stockings and a white starched apron and cap behind a desk. "I'm Mrs Belinda Bowler," she said, "I have an appointment with the gynaecologist at 10am."

The nurse examined her list. "Yes, take a seat, Mrs Bowler."

This she did and was later shown into the examination room. At last, to her relief, her ordeal was over but the 'internal' hadn't shown up anything that might be causing her infertility. The gynaecologist seemed to think there was no real reason why she shouldn't conceive eventually and advised her to be patient.

Just after this Roger came home on leave once again and told her that he'd managed to arrange married quarters for them both at his camp in Lincolnshire. She supposed she was pleased about this, but not about having to leave her job at the Servicemen's Club which she was enjoying, or saying goodbye to her good friend, Olivia, though they both intended to keep in touch with letters.

A few weeks later saw her and Roger in their first home, if you could call the prefabricated hut a home. Some evenings he would take her to the Officers' Mess to dances or just for a few drinks. At the dances, he would continue with the same trick as he had in Oxford, which didn't please her. When she told him this he just brushed aside her complaints. At the Mess she would come into contact with the other wives. On the surface they all seemed friendly enough, but she felt out of place amongst the middle-class English girls, with their accents sounding as if they were chewing a plum. Then there was always someone announcing that they were expecting a baby. Though no one exactly said anything, she felt they were all looking at her, her tummy especially, and wondering when she was going to announce that she too, was expecting. Of course, this never happened. What especially hurt was when one of the wives who already had children said, "Oh, gosh, I'm 'b' pregnant again!"

This made her heart bleed, she'd have swapped places with them in an instance.

There was one bright spot for her at Roger's camp - one

that had been quite unexpected but certainly was welcome. This was meeting up again with Gillian Adams whom she had last seen before 'The Denver' went down. Gillian had gone with the other nurses in an earlier lifeboat to the one she was in. Belinda had been shopping in the village. Entering the Post Office to post a letter to Mom and Pop back home she'd felt a tap on her shoulder. "If it isn't Belinda Bowler," said a female voice with a strong American accent.

She had looked around in surprise. Who was speaking to her? To her disbelief she recognised Gillian. "You're alive!"

"Of course, I'm alive," she laughed. "Did you think me dead?"

"I didn't know, but I'm glad you're not."

"Me, too!"

"So what happened to you?" asked Belinda, as she paid for an airmail stamp and passed her letter over the counter to the Post Mistress. .She turned back to Gillian. "And more importantly, what are you doing here?"

Gillian tossed back her blonde curls.

They left the shop together. "Go on. I'm in no hurry."

"Okay then, well, after drifting for several days we were picked up by another American ship, 'The George Washington' was en route for Liverpool. Once in Liverpool I heard they were short of nurses at their Mill Road Hospital. Liverpool was badly bombed in '41 and '42, and a lot of the nurses and doctors as well as the patients were killed. Feeling that perhaps I could be of use in Liverpool I got permission from the American authorities, applied to the hospital and was taken on. Shortly after this, I nursed a woman who was in hospital with a grumbling appendicitis. She had a visitor, her nephew Jimmy, a young RAF pilot. We fell in love and married, and when he was transferred to this camp, I came here with him.

"Well, it's wonderful to see you again, hon."

"It's great to see you, too."

So after this, they had quite a bit to do with each other, especially as Roger and Jimmy seemed to get on well. They had some good times as a foursome in the Officers' Mess. Belinda felt more at ease with Gillian, and not at all as she felt when she had to come into contact with the middle- class English wives whom she'd soon realised liked her no more than she liked them. With the two girls becoming close friends they often spent the hours together while their husbands were flying on 'ops over Germany.

Time passed. Eventually Roger was once more on leave and they were again stopping at his home in Oxford. While there, she visited Doctor Green. "Still, no sign of a happy event?" he asked.

She swallowed the lump in her throat. "No."

"I see. Well, I think we should arrange a D & C for you at the Radcliffe. "

"What's a D & C?"

"It's dilation of the cervix, my dear. You will have to stay overnight at the hospital. It could be fibroids that are causing your problem."

"Fibroids! But I'm only nineteen. I thought it was older women who had fibroids?"

"Not necessarily, my dear. Should fibroids be found and removed, you could then conceive."

"Oh, I hope so doctor, I really hope so."

"If it isn't fibroids, then perhaps we'll have to get your husband to supply a sample of his sperm."

So an appointment at the hospital was made for her to coincide with Roger's next leave. She went in full of trepidation. Would this D & C be painful? She wasn't sure she could handle a lot of pain, but she was desperate to get a baby, and so she knew was Roger. With constantly risking his life he wanted to make sure that if he should get killed he would leave a descendant on this earth. As it happened this D & C wasn't too bad as she was put to sleep and when she came round her ordeal was over and she was being wheeled back to the ward.

Just after this Dr Green came to visit her. "As I

suspected," he said, "the surgeon did find a couple of fibroids which he successfully removed. We can only hope this will do the trick and you'll soon be pushing around a pram."

At Dr Green's words, Belinda visualised a pram containing a dear little baby who rather resembled Roger. For the rest of this leave, she was walking on air. But when her next period was due her hopes were dashed, as it came as it always did.

It was almost a year later with still no sign of a baby that she again met up with Hank. She had gone to visit Olivia at the Servicemen's club and who should be there playing a game of pool, but Hank. "Hank! It's you, isn't it?"

He turned and grinned widely. "Belinda!"

She smiled back at him. "I didn't expect to see you again, at least not so soon. I thought you'd still be away, wherever it was that you were sent to."

"'North Africa, that's where we ended up. Nothing but heat, flies and sand there. I can't say I was sorry to leave. The official end of 'Operation Torch' was on the 15th of May 1943. I'm back now at Didcot. So how are you?"

"Not so bad." They sat down at a table and chatted. The heat of North Africa hadn't suited him and he'd suffered heatstroke more than once. She knew she'd really missed him, and after that whenever she was in Oxford she would phone Hank at Didcot, then making some excuse to Roger that she was going to meet Olivia she would meet Hank instead and they would spend a couple of hours together.

CHAPTER NINE

Susan had decided to marry Sam. Why shouldn't she? After all, she had lost Roger for ever. The American had stolen him from her. Though knowing Roger like she did she didn't think he would have put up much of a fight to stay true to her. Sam was so different to Roger, he seemed to be really in love with her and perhaps that was the most important thing. Better for the man to be the keenest. She wanted a husband and a home of her own. She wanted children too, and you needed a husband to have children. She was fond of Sam, and she wasn't certain that she'd ever want to be madly in love again. It was too painful. Sam was safe, he would make a good caring husband and father for her children.

So a few days later, she almost asked Sam to marry her. They were strolling along the tow-path beside the river. It was a lovely day, the sun was shining and the weeping willows on the other side of the river dipped down gracefully into the water. On both sides of the grass verges of the river bank, courting couples were laid in each other's arms.

Sam was delighted, and kissing her soundly, swung her off her feet. "I wasn't certain you loved me? I thought you might still be pining for that Roger? "

She bit her lip. "Not likely! Of course I love you. Roger's in the past. You are my future. "

"That's all right then," he said relieved. "If that's what you really want, we'll be married as soon as it can be arranged."

He did all the right things, asked her dad for his permission. Her father willing gave it, as he liked Sam, though he did say when they were on their own, "Are you sure, love, marriage is for the rest of your life, you're not just on the rebound?"

She didn't like lying, especially to her father, but she couldn't tell him the truth, that her dad had read her thoughts – that she was definitely far from certain whether this might be the case. "No, of course not," she said adamantly.

"I hope that is the truth you're telling me as you could regret marrying without love later on."

Susan crossed her fingers behind her back. "I know that Dad. I'm not stupid. I want to marry Sam, he's definitely the man for me, I'm certain we'll be happy together."

Her father had to be satisfied with that.

Sam took her to Rowells & Sons in the High Street and bought her a diamond engagement ring, which he proudly pushed onto the third finger of her left hand. Her parents put an announcement in the Oxford Times, they also gave them a party in their front room to celebrate the engagement to which they invited their friends, the Bowlers, and Sam's parents, Mr & Mrs Walker who lived in Headington. She had met them before and found them as pleasant as their son. They were delighted too with the proposed addition to their family.

Sam's parents were Church of England. And as Susan was no longer attending the Baptist Chapel in case she might run into Roger and his new wife, the wedding was arranged to be held at St. Andrew's Church in Headington on Saturday the 11th of October 1943. They were to live with Sam's parents. - making their home in the Walker's front room and Sam's bedroom for the time being. Later, Sam hoped to save up a deposit so they could buy a house of their own. Although, so far Oxford hadn't been bombed, housing, especially Council houses was in short supply. Newly-weds had to be on the housing list for quite some time and also have at least two children to qualify.

So the wedding went off well. Susan wore her cousin's wedding dress and Sam, his fireman's dress uniform, and the reception was held in Susan's parents' front room, with the combined friends and families of the couple giving up some of their rations to supply the food for the happy event.

But in the church as Sam, with a tender look of love on

his face, slipped his late grandmother's gold band onto the third finger of her left hand, she felt a sudden pang. Had she done the right thing in marrying Sam? Was she being fair to him feeling as she still did about Roger?

Time passed, married life was all right, even the intimate side, although, if she was to be honest with herself, there wasn't really that much excitement. Her heart didn't beat faster as it had with Roger when Sam took her in his arms and kissed her. There was no magic.

Then she found she was pregnant.

CHAPTER TEN

It was just another 'op – exactly the same at first as so many others had been before. An hour after take-off they were flying at about 12,000 feet, on course direct for Berlin. They flew on for three hours, all quiet and undisturbed, apart from a few searchlights which tried to pierce the thick cloud below. The flak over the coastline was clearly seen. Roger's thoughts drifted away from the job in hand – to Susan of all people, well, it was only natural he supposed they had been close for a considerably amount of time. He recalled seeing her in the distance on his last leave in Oxford – and registering the swell of her belly. With a pang he'd realised she was pregnant. Of course, he'd known she was now married. This had occurred some months ago. His mother had a wedding photo of her and the fireman, she'd made no effort to hide it – in fact, the opposite. She had bought a frame for it and placed it on the wall in their passage. Perhaps she thought the photo might upset him, and if it did, well, serve him right! He had to admit he wasn't completely unmoved. He'd certainly felt strangely annoyed with Belinda, when, before the photograph had been placed in a frame and hung up she had pushed it aside after pointing to the fireman and remarking in a derogative manner, "Second best!"

And then for him to see Susan pregnant. That child should have been his! He'd tried and tried to get Belinda pregnant. Nothing had happened. They both wanted a baby so badly. Not only that, but a baby could settle her down, he knew she was homesick, missing her family in the U.S. which was understandable. He shook himself. Good Heavens, this wasn't the time to dwell on his personal problems – they were about to bomb Germany. He realised they were now flying in a clear sky lit by searchlights, fighter flares and explosions. He quickly checked his calculations; knew that this moment was the correct bombing time. He spoke into his radio to tell the bomb-aimer to drop the bombs, which the bomb-aimer did. All seemed well as far as this was concerned. Beneath the clouds the night sky was lit up by Berlin's burning suburbs. Now, they could return to Blighty, where Roger knew a warm bed with a warm body in it was waiting for him.

Then to his disbelief, from nowhere appeared enemy fighters – a few second later, their plane was hit. Ear-piercing yells sounded, first from the tail-gunner in his turret, then by the other gunner in his turret, finally from the rest of the crew, followed by deathly silence. Roger saw that the pilot, flight- engineer, wireless-operator, bomb-aimer and the two gunners were slumped over. Horrified, he realised that everyone, apart from himself was dead!

He knew he'd have to take over flying the plane – he'd no choice, not if he wanted to survive. With trembling fingers he began to unbuckle himself, and seconds later succeeded, but something was blocking his way, some debris caused by the plane being hit – his right foot was trapped. He tried to unzip his flying boot to release his foot but the zip was stuck. He struggled with it, fruitlessly, his heart beating like a drum beneath his chest. Oh, God, he was going to die too if he couldn't get to where the pilot was slumped over the controls in time. He began to pray, harder than he ever had before. "Our Father, who art in Heaven, hallowed....."

At last, after what seemed a lifetime, the zip moved and he was able to slip his foot out of the boot. He squeezed his way, averting his eyes from the mangled bloodied remains of his friends, to where, Jock, the pilot was slumped with blank eyes, a great gash in his forehead and blood all over his flying clothes. He tried to move him, but couldn't, Jock was far too heavy to shift easily being six foot four tall and burly with it. He tried again, and again, and at last with a great effort managed to pull Jock out of his seat.

By this time, the plane was heading towards the British

coastline. He slid into the vacant seat, and grabbed the joystick, putting his feet on the foot controls and only just in time as with a whine the plane was nose diving towards the ground. He struggled with the joystick and as he did so his previous life flashed before him. At last, the plane's flight levelled out. He gasped with relief, and inside his helmet his face was all wet.

Somehow, he managed to reach their airfield where the plane bumped along the runway before finally coming to a halt. He had landed the plane, how he didn't quite know. Stiffly, he climbed from it, his legs so shaky that he could hardly keep his balance and had to be supported by two of the several ground crew who'd immediately appeared. They helped him along to the Medical Centre, where he would be examined by the M.O. But he soon realised he had more to cope with than just keeping upright as when he turned his head he saw others of the ground crew begin to wash out the bits of bodies from the plane with hose-pipes. At this gruesome sight bile oozed up into his mouth and he was violently sick.

He remembered little after that, everything, even de-briefing and being examined by the M.O. was a daze, filled with nightmares of that flight every time he put his head to his pillow. He knew he was quieter than usual as Belinda often complained of the fact.

* * *

The weeks passed, and to his relief the subsequent 'ops he went on were uneventful compared to that horrific one. He never said too much to Belinda about how he had landed the plane, though he knew the story of it must have been all round the camp. Then to his astonishment, he received a letter from Buckingham Palace. It appeared he was to be awarded the DFC, the Distinguished Flying Cross, by King George V1 on the 16th of May, 1944, and was allowed to take three guests with him to witness the ceremony.

He knew Belinda was thrilled at this, as his wife, she automatically expected to be one of the guests to accompany him to Buckingham Palace, and the thought of visiting the palace and seeing King George himself was something she couldn't stop talking about. So much so, he imagined that all the wives of the other RAF personnel that she came into contact with must have got rather fed up with her.

They were to travel by train from Oxford to London on the morning of the 16th of May – Oxford being only about an hour's train journey from London, accompanied also by Roger's mother whom it had been decided should be his other guest – his father being unable to get time off work to attend. Roger had never before seen his mother so smartly attired. She wore a pale cream woollen costume that she must have either borrowed from someone or got from a second-hand shop. On her head she wore a matching hat with a little net veil over her forehead. Belinda, too, he imagined wouldn't let him down as regards her appearance. She had borrowed a green dress and matching coat from a friend she knew from her time at the Servicemen's Club.

Their train steamed into Paddington Station and they alighted, but when they reached the Underground his mother rather showed herself up by loudly refusing to go on the escalator - she never having seen one before. In fact, he and Belinda had to take an arm each to help her on, and off again at the other end. After a short ride on an Underground train, they exited from the station, and made their way towards the palace. There were signs everywhere of the war – brown paper strips up at the windows, and piles of sandbags at street corners. But the worst thing of all was the bombed buildings. Roofless and windowless, revealing, a picture on a wall, a baby's cot, in and half out of what was once a bedroom. Roger's mother put her hand over her nose, "What a stench. Is it drains, do you think?"

"Could be dead bodies," said Roger.

His mother shivered. "Do you think so?"

He didn't reply. It was more than likely.

They walked along the road adjacent to the Thames and London Bridge. Small ships pulled against their anchors, and several of the ships wore battle scars where canon shells had damaged the metal plating high in the bow. Out in the mainstream laden larger barges lay lower in the water. The sun had broken through the clouds and it lit up the quayside and the tall cranes and shone down on the white stonework of the Tower of London, and Tower Bridge. At last they reached the palace. By this time his mother was in a right tizzy, she'd always been awestruck of the 'gentry' as she called the middle-classes from her time in Service and the thought of entering Buckingham Palace and seeing royalty at close quarters was almost too much for her. The place was packed, there were 120 recipients at each investiture, every one of them with three guests. One of the gentlemen ushers approached Roger and his party and told Belinda and his mother to follow him, which they did.

He was then briefed by someone from the Lord Chancellor's office: what he needed to know as regards his behaviour when approaching the king and then exiting backwards.

In the ballroom, Roger's mother and wife joined the other excited, chattering guests while Roger joined the rest of the nervous recipients. An orchestra, the Band of the Household Division was playing. He looked around, he had never seen such a huge room before. There were dozens of large ornate chandeliers with crystal droplets hanging from the ceiling and tall velvet curtained windows. In front of where the guests were sitting was a red velvet dais beneath a giant, domed velvet canopy. He supposed this was where the King would stand to present the medals. At this thought his stomach churned and the palms of his hands felt damp.

There was a sudden hush, and the King entered the ballroom, escorted by the Lord Chamberlain, and attended by two Ghurkha orderly officers. Already on duty on the dais were five members of the King's Body Guard of the Yeoman of the Guard. After the National Anthem was played the Lord Chamberlain came and stood to the right of His Majesty and announced the names of each recipient in turn and the achievement for which they were being decorated. Eventually, his name was called out, "ROGER BOWLER."

He stepped forward and moved towards the King – a man of average height and build and with dark hair.

"Roger Bowler, a navigator, landed his Lancaster single-handed when all the rest of the crew were killed," said the Lord Chamberlain.

"Well, done," said King George, rather carefully Roger realized, His Majesty appearing to have a slight speech impediment. He firmly pinned the DFC onto the tunic of Roger's uniform.

"Thank you," said Roger, and when the King's hand was offered to him, he shook it, before bowing and exiting backwards to loud applause.

Afterwards, in an anteroom where drinks and refreshments were served, he, Belinda and his mother examined the medal. It was made of silver with a distinctive diagonal blue stripe and dated 1944.

"You must be feeling very proud of yourself, hon? To think I'm married to a war hero," gushed Belinda.

His mother kissed his cheek. "Yes, well, done, Son."

Roger swallowed. He didn't know how he felt for sure, he certainly didn't feel like much of a hero, all he knew was that he would never forget those good mates he had lost on that 'op. They were the REAL Heroes.

* * *

On the way back to get their train at Paddington Station they suddenly heard the unearthly wail of a siren.

"Oh, no," exclaimed Agatha. "That's all we need to be caught up in an air raid!" She began to shake and struggle with her gas mask case. This would be the first time she had actually worn it. Hearing a droning overhead, she looked up fearfully, seeing through the Perspex window the shapes of planes, her imagination supplying the swastikas. Something was falling with a whine – bombs? She looked around in terror and confusion. Where was the nearest shelter? Oh, God, they were going to be killed!

"Come on, Mum," said Roger, "we need to get to the Underground. We can shelter there," and both he and Belinda each grabbed one of her arms and began to haul her along. "We're almost there."

Agatha gasped, "Not so fast, I'm getting out of breath!"

"Better to be out of breath, Mum, than dead!"

People were shouting and running past them – young mothers desperately wheeling prams at breakneck speed, or half dragging sobbing children. A young lad with concertina socks appeared with a yelping mongrel on the end of a piece of string. A bus ground to a halt, and all the passengers piled off, and like the others, ran past them. An old man, hobbling on a walking stick, turned back, cap awry, his head nodding in his gas mask as he yelled at her. "Come on, Mother. Get under cover!" He shook his fist at the sky. "Bloody Huns! Trying to catch us on the hop like this. Usually the bastards don't put in an appearance 'till it's completely dark. They'll be coming in broad daylight next."

At last, they reached the Underground Station and everyone hurried into it. In the distance Agatha could see an escalator with a great crowd of people pouring onto it. She flinched, she knew that she would have to follow their example. Suddenly, she heard an ear-piercing scream as a woman tripped, toppled over and fell from top to bottom. No one stopped to try and help her. No one could, there was just too many people and having no choice they all walked over her. When she herself reached where the twisted body lay, like everyone else, she had to step on her, too – and was sickened when she felt something squashy beneath her shoe.

Eventually, reaching a platform where they were to

shelter, they were all crowded together on the hard narrow benches, the women trying to comfort the terrified children., everyone sweating in their gas masks, as they listened with bated breath to the sinister throbbing overhead, the crump of bombs and the ack-ack guns' reply, hoping and praying that none of the bombs would have their number on it. After a particularly horrendous explosion which sounded like hundreds of tea trays clattering downstairs, or cart loads of coal being tipped into cellars, she noticed Roger's expression which said clearly: This has brought it home to me what it's like to be on the other side. I can visualise now what those civilians in Germany must suffer when we drop our bombs on them!

A WVS tea trolley appeared. From a huge green aluminium teapot, tea was poured into thick white cups and offered around. Having taken off her gas mask, Agatha took the proffered cup in trembling hands, but the hot sweet tea (the supposedly cheering Rosy Lee) did nothing to sooth her apprehension..

At last, the All Clear sounded. Stiffly, everyone got to their feet, and Roger, Belinda, and Agatha, she having to brave a couple more escalators, before getting onto an Underground train, found their way to Paddington Station where they could catch their train back to Oxford. Alighting at Oxford Station, Agatha turned to Roger. "Well, that's the last time I ever go to London. I couldn't face something like that again, even for a thousand pound fortune."

* * *

He and Belinda had only been back at the camp in Lincolnshire for a few days when Roger, to his disbelief heard the siren wailing with the same unearthly cry that he'd heard while in London.

Everyone looked askance at each other. "What on earth?"

They were being briefed by Wing Commander Collins as regards their approaching mission that night. Realisation hitting them, everyone leapt from their seats and dashed outside to stare up at the sky. The noise of throbbing engines filled the air, and everywhere Roger looked people were milling about in confusion. There was a German plane overhead. Their airfield had never been bombed before, so why now? They had no time to think about it as he saw bombs, with a whine, were falling from it. Everyone, Roger included, threw themselves flat on the ground as a bomb landed on one of their aircraft on the nearby runway and exploded with a deafening bang. Pieces of shrapnel from the plane flew through the air towards them and a sharp, dagger-like piece pierced the forehead of Pete, whom he knew slightly who was lying beside him. Pete screamed in agony and his eyeballs protruded, seconds he made a funny gurgling sound and then all went quiet. Horrified, Roger realised he was dead.

He saw another bomb descending, it hit one of the huts. The explosion caused it to disintegrate with a loud rumble into a pile of rubble and broken shards of wood. Seeing this, he was glad that Belinda and Gillian had decided to go into Lincoln on a shopping trip this morning. At least they were safe, but what would they think on their return if the camp was completely demolished and everyone was dead?

He hoped and prayed it wouldn't come to that!

Then he noticed one of the R.A.F. cooks - the one who always gave him extra helpings. He was lain on the ground some distance away, near to the wreckage that had once been a hut. Was he dead? As if in reply, the man moaned and moved slightly. .He was obviously alive, he must have been stunned by the blast, but he mightn't be alive much longer if another bomb should fall onto the adjoining hut unless he was got into cover. As Roger mulled this over he saw another bomb descending – heading for the second hut. Hastily, he scrambled to his feet and quickly ran over to where the cook was lying. He picked him up, thankful that he was no heavyweight, and carried him out of harm's way. And only just in time, as the bomb hit the hut and exploded with a loud bang, turning it into just rubble as with the first hut.

At last, the plane flew away – leaving utter devastation behind it – as well as several dead. Medics then appeared and took the cook to their Sickbay, where he recovered after a day or two.

Roger went to visit him. "You're a hero," said the cook, shaking him by the hand.

He brushed his praise aside. "It was no more than what anyone else would do!"

* * *

It was just after Roger and Belinda had returned to Lincolnshire that Wilfred announced he was to be sent up to London to repair the water mains in the bombed buildings.

"What! Definitely not! I don't want you to go," said Agatha. "London is too dangerous, you could get killed in the bombing. I couldn't bear that!" She recalled the time, barely a week previously when they themselves were caught in an air raid in London. She'd never forget the sight of that woman who had fallen on the escalator or the feel of her shattered body under her shoe.

"You've just been up there, Mum, to see our Roger get his medal."

"Of course, I was thrilled to see him receiving his award, but apart from that I wish that I hadn't! As I've told you we got caught in a fluke air raid. It is usually at night that the Luftwaffe bombers come over. The damage they have done to our capital city. You should see the bombed buildings, smell the stench everywhere. " She bit her lip, they were lucky in Oxford – at least, so far!

Wilfred swallowed. He'd guessed he'd get opposition to this from his mother. "I can't refuse. There's a war on, you know."

75

"I know that, but you're only nineteen."

"So I might be, but I could have been called up at eighteen and sent abroad to fight for King and Country. It's only because I'm in a reserved occupation that I haven't been."

"He's right, Mother," said George.

"Huh! How long have you got to go for?"

"I'm not sure, Mum, until things die down in London, I suppose."

She turned to George. "You don't want him to go to London, do you?"

"Of course, I don't. But you heard what Wilfred has said, he's got to. He's got no choice in the matter. We'll just have to pray that he'll be safe, pray like we do every night for our Roger's safety. Unfortunately, that's all we can do."

"I don't like it!"

"Well, I don't like it either, but I don't suppose all the other parents of young men like their boys being sent off to become cannon fodder. War's a terrible thing. Please God, when this one ends there'll be no more."

"That's what everyone hoped for in 1918, but only twenty-one years later, the idiots in both governments, Germany and ours, decide on another."

George put his arm around Agatha. "You're upset, love, and its only to be expected with us hearing about our Wilfred. Now, I'll make you a nice cup of tea – it'll help you feel a little better." He lifted the big black kettle off the hob and placing a teaspoon of tea leaves into the teapot poured on hot water.

As she took the cup of tea from him, she said. "I wish I could give a cuppa to that swine, Hitler. Tea with some rat poisoning in it."

* * *

A few days later, Wilfred left for London.

Agatha was on tenterhooks. Would he be all right? Please God, he would. He said he'd write as often as he could so she would know. If only they could be like the rich people in their big houses – people like those she had slaved for when she was little more than a child, and for barely more than her keep. The 'gentry', she was certain, would have a telephone in their houses, maybe more than one. With a telephone her Wilfred could ring her every evening and keep her mind at rest.

CHAPTER ELEVEN

Sharp pains in Susan's tummy woke her. She nudged Sam. He moaned, but never stirred. She nudged him again, harder this time. "Wake up! I think the baby's coming."

"What! He hastily sat up. "Are you sure?"

"I think so, as much as I can be. I've never had one before, but there's blood on our bottom sheet."

He swung his legs over his side of the bed, and hastily stood up. "Shall I ring the hospital?"

"Yes." She winced and put her hand onto her tummy, "It's hurting again!"

He dressed hurriedly and went downstairs, reaching for his overcoat from the peg in the passage, and slipping it on.

The front door banged- to. He ran up the street to the phone box.

Meanwhile, Susan had got dressed herself and downstairs, carrying the bag she had got ready for her visit to the hospital. She was overdue according to the dates she'd been given. They had told her to come in tomorrow morning (Sunday) to be started off. She'd not known what that meant, she'd only hoped it wouldn't be too painful.

The front door opened, and he dashed in, gasping for breath.

"What did they say?"

"They said to get a taxi and come up straight away. I've phoned one it should be here in a few minutes. "

"Good!" She bent over and bit her lips as a fresh lot pains stabbed at her. To her relief, they faded. "They're coming closer together now. Hurry up taxi! I don't want to give birth on the lino in our passage!"

As she spoke she heard a car slow down and stop outside "It's here," she said, relieved.

Sam locked the door behind them, and they both got in. "The Radcliffe, Nuffield Maternity Home, Walton Street," he said.

"Right, Guv'" said the taxi driver. He put his foot on the accelerator and the car sped away – so swiftly that Susan wondered if he was afraid that she might give birth in his taxi and he'd have to clean up the mess.

Within a few minutes, they were there. They went inside, and to the reception desk. "I'm Mrs Walker.," she said, "Mrs Susan Walker. I'm booked in here. I think my baby's coming!"

The receptionist rang a bell. A midwife in a white cap and apron appeared. She spoke to Sam. "You'll have to wait in the Waiting Room. Soon as I've settled your wife in, I'll take you to it."

"Thank you," said Sam. His expression revealing he would have rather stayed with Susan.

She turned. "I'll take you to the Delivery Room. She set off, Susan following her. What was going to happen to her? She was very apprehensive. At least, she wouldn't have to be started off now, whatever that was, and as she had 'started' on her own, would that make things easier for her? She hoped so.

There was a high hospital bed in the Delivery Room. How on earth am I going to climb up into that with my huge tummy?

"Get undressed and put this on," said the midwife, handing her a white gown that fastened at the back.

Susan put on the gown, which the midwife fastened for her, and with the midwife's help, managed to clamber up onto the bed.

"I'll need to shave you," said the midwife

She blenched at the sight of a wicked-looking cut-throat razor, thinking, Shave me? Where? She soon found out and was rather embarrassed as her private parts were deftly shorn. .Meanwhile, the pains were becoming closer and closer. She noticed a glass jar on the windowsill containing instruments. Long, sharp, wicked looking instruments. Oh, God, I hope they're not going to use them on me! She imagined them probing at her and shivered, praying that they wouldn't need to use them. She was sure that she would die if they did. Fortunately, for Susan, they didn't!

A couple of hours later, having been left on her own for quite long periods of time, the midwife only popping in to see her occasionally, she suddenly remembered Sam. When the midwife reappeared she asked her if her husband was still in the Waiting Room?

"Is he still there?" she replied, surprised.

"I think so."

She went off and found him. He was sitting in the dark as the bulb in the room was dead.

"How is she?" he asked.

"Okay, but it'll be some time yet. You'd best go home and get some sleep, there's nothing you can do here. Ring in the morning, we might be able to tell you something by then."

"Thank you," he replied, and left.

She returned to Susan. "He's gone. I told him to ring in later."

By now the pains were almost constant. She grimaced and put down the mouthpiece of the gas- and-air machine that had been placed by the bedside for her to use to ease her discomfort. "I thought something like this machine would make you feel light-headed. I don't feel any different."

The midwife examined the machine. "I'm sorry, dear, but it's empty. We've had a run on it tonight."

After several hours, Susan was told she was almost ready to give birth. "When you get your next contraction, Push, Push!"

She did just that. "I can see the head. Not long now. "

There came another even stronger contraction, and she pushed, and pushed as if she was pushing out a huge thick door that wouldn't budge. Every sinew strained, the pain was enormous. Suddenly, the door gave way and out slithered a baby.

"It's a boy," exclaimed the midwife, holding him up and briskly smacking his bottom. At this they heard a furious cry. She laughed. "He sound a bit annoyed at having to leave his warm nest."

Susan lay back, exhausted but happy. Her baby was born.

A little while later, having cleaned him up, the midwife placed him, wrapped up securely in a white towel, into her arms. She pressed a gentle kiss on his little forehead, then examined him, counting his little fingers and toes. He was perfect. He didn't seem to resemble Sam all that much. He was more like her with the small fair tufts of hair on his head. She studied him closely. He should have been Roger's! She didn't hate him for letting her down like he had. Didn't hold it against him. She hoped he was well and safe when airborne. If she blamed anyone, she blamed that Yankee – she was a conniving madam. Well, she was sure that the woman would get her punishment sometime, though perhaps she would never know if she did. She knew she still had feelings for Roger. It wasn't fair to Sam, but she couldn't help it.

Her baby was taken to the nursery to sleep with all the other new babies, while she managed to get a sleep herself.

Sam rang an hour or so later. The receptionist told the midwife and she passed his message on to her. He'd said he was thrilled to be a dad, and that he would be coming to see her and his son at visiting time.

She stayed in hospital for ten days which was normal for all women after giving birth. The midwives taught her to breast-feed – which was best for her baby to give him a good start in life. Not only that, but when the baby suckled she could feel her womb contracting, which she'd been told would help her to get back her pre-pregnancy figure. They also supervised her bathing him. She was glad of this as being an only child she had had no experience of babies. By the time she went home she was more confident at handling John, the name they'd decided to call him.

CHAPTER TWELVE

Sixteen-year-old, Alec, wasn't at all pleased to see Roger and his wife, Belinda, back again on leave at their house. Well, he was pleased to see Roger, but not that 'Yankee' as he called her to himself. He didn't think she was treating his brother right, she was definitely meeting that American, Hank on the sly; whom she'd had the cheek to bring home with her on several occasions. One day, when he was repairing some electrical wiring on the roof of a house in St Ebbes, to his astonishment he had spotted his sister-in-law and Hank walking along the pavement on the opposite side of the street with their arms all around each other. To him, that could only mean one thing, they were making a fool of his brother and carrying on with each other, where, or how, he didn't know, but he felt sure that this was the case.

He knew his mother wasn't all that keen on Belinda either. When Roger and the Yankee came and stopped in their house, she never offered to help Mum with any of the chores before going off somewhere with Roger. Unlike Susan, Susan would have insisted on helping Mum. She always had whenever she'd visited. Even when Roger had been adamant that he wanted them to go off somewhere immediately. Not so Belinda. He had seen Mum's lips tighten on more than one occasion when she was left yet again with a huge pile of washing up to see to.

Then there was the time when she had caused a big row. It was a Sunday morning. They were all downstairs after having breakfast. He'd decided to go upstairs to his room. She must have decided to go upstairs at the same time. It was her habit to come down for breakfast before dressing, wearing just a housecoat over her nightclothes. She was in front of him as they climbed the stairs and he noticed that the bottom of her long housecoat was trailing over the lino stair-covering. Without thinking, he'd pulled up the hem of the housecoat hoping to avert an accident.

To his astonishment, she'd yelled out, "You pervert, you! How dare you make a pass at me! I'm your brother's wife. You're disgusting, that's what you are."

Astonished, not really knowing what a pervert was, he had mumbled that he'd just thought she might trip on the hem of the housecoat, but with a face like thunder she'd pushed past him and stormed back to the living room to where Roger and his mum and dad were still seated at the table.

Alec followed after her. He'd not been trying to make a pass at her, he wouldn't, surely his mum and dad would realise that.

"Your brother's a pervert," she screeched. "He's only pulled up the bottom of my housecoat hoping to see what he shouldn't, I reckon."

"I'm not what you said I was, whatever that is. I wouldn't do that anyway," said Alec.

Roger spluttered over his cup of tea. "What?"

"He's only tried it on with me."

At Belinda's words, Roger's mouth tightened and with clenched fists he turned on Alec. "I'll give you such a pasting you little sod," he hissed, "have you no respect, she's your sister-in-law, for God's sake."

"But Roger, it's all a mistake," Alec attempted to explain. "I never meant anything by it. I lifted the hem of her housecoat that much is true, but I thought she was going to trip over it."

"Liar!" exclaimed Belinda.

"I'm not!"

By this time Roger's dad was on his feet. "Now, lads, fighting never solved anything. I'm sure it's all a storm in a teacup, if Alec says he never meant anything by it, then he didn't. You should believe him. Surely you must know that Alec isn't the sort to try and seduce anyone. "

Roger grimaced. "Believe him! Not believe my wife? Fat chance!" He raised his fists in a threatening manner.

At this, she smirked.

Their mother had also risen from her chair. "No, Roger,

don't! Don't hit him!"

But Roger was too angry to heed her. "I will if I want to!" His fist shot out aimed at Alec, but his dad hurriedly moved forward to protect his younger son and got in the way of the fierce blow which landed on the side of his face with a sickening thud. "Ouch!" He slapped a hand over his stinging cheek.

Roger's anger died as quickly as it had developed. "Oh, Dad, I'm so sorry, that wasn't meant for you."

"I know that," said his father, still rubbing his cheek.

"Why did you get in the way?"

"Do you need to ask? Violence never solved anything. Now, both of you shake hands!"

Reluctantly, both Roger and Alec, looking rather sheepish, did just that.

As he climbed the stairs to his room once more Alec recalled that smirk on Belinda's face. Could Roger be getting cold feet as regards leaving England and going to America with the Yankee once the war was over? This mightn't be too far off as the recent Battle of Britain had gone in their favour. He was sure she'd used this incident as a means to an end – to hopefully turn Roger against his own family so he would be more amenable to leaving the U.K., he imagined she must be missing her own family and the way of life she was used to, but even so.

The blow left a dark bruise on his father's cheek which took a week or more to fade, this meant that every time Alec registered it, he disliked the Yankee even more than he had before.

* * *

George felt apprehensive when he went to work at the Railway Workshops the following day. He expected ragging from his workmates because of the huge purple bruise on his right cheek. His expectations came true.

"Wow! That's a beauty, George. Has the missus been knocking you about?" exclaimed Jack who worked next to him.

"Of course not, she wouldn't do something like that. I bumped into the door."

"That's a good excuse, they all say that. Who really hit you?"

"No one." He wasn't going to wash his dirty linen in public, admit that he'd been hit by his own son – accidentally, he knew, but he wasn't going to tell the truth of what really happened to anyone."

"So what have you been doing?" asked Jim, a workmate of many years, but a gossip-monger. He could have been a woman the way he liked gossiping about everybody's business.

"Nothing."

"Bloody liar! It must be something bad. Have you been carrying on with another woman? Did her husband give you what for?" chuckled Jack.

"Of course not. There is no woman, or husband. I'd not do something like that, anyway."

"So it's the missus then. You must have done something bad for her to hit you."

"She didn't!"

"I say, she did. "

"No."

"A battered husband, then. That's what you are."

All George's other workmates laughed at this.

"Never mind what George is," interrupted their foreman suddenly appearing from behind a milling machine. "It's time you all got some work done!"

They all hastily got on with what they were supposed to be doing.

As George worked on his surface grinder, he wished for a hundredth time that Roger hadn't gone to America and got tangled up with an American. He would have married Susan if he hadn't. She would have been a much better wife for him. He'd heard she'd just had a baby – a little boy. That child would have been his and Agatha's grandson. When he got bigger he could have gone fishing with him, perhaps helped him on his allotment. He and the child would no doubt, as time passed, become very close. As things were, if Belinda did ever have a baby, there'd been no sign of one even though she and Roger had been married for some time – with her being a foreigner and naturally wanting to return to America after the war – no doubt nagging Roger so that he agreed that they would go, they'd take any child they might have with them and he and Agatha would never see it again! He supposed he couldn't really blame the girl for wanting to return home, but if she had made trouble on purpose for her own ends, well, that was unforgivable.

It was ten days or more before the bruise faded and he felt less self-conscious, but the memory of the row which had caused it took a lot longer to fade.

CHAPTER THIRTEEN

Wilfred had settled into his digs in Shoreditch. He shared a room with three other apprentice plumbers, who like himself had also been sent to the Capital to repair the damaged water mains. Their room was pleasant with three single beds covered with patchwork quilts – there was even an inside lavatory which had to be an improvement to what he was used to - but the view from the window only revealed a little backyard and dustbins, which, in the middle of the night, if they weren't disturbed by the Luftwaffe and their bombs and so needed to shelter in the Underground; stray cats in the area would knock the lids off and disturb their sleep.

He got on well with his room-mates, Tom, Harry and Jack. And in their off duty time they would visit The Windmill Theatre so they could whistle at the flimsily clad girls, and enjoy the repartee of the comedians. Their landlady, Mrs Foster, who by her comfortable figure, revealed that she fed herself and them, too, very well indeed, despite the rationing.

One afternoon, repairing the water mains beneath a demolished street, Wilfred heard a ticking noise. What was that?"

With one hand he carefully brushed away the dirt and debris in front of him and saw to his horror something that looked like a bomb – a V-1 Flying bomb that was known also as a buzz bomb or doodlebug?

He lifted his head as high as he could and looked over the top of the pit he was in and shouted, "Help! I think I've found a buzz bomb – get help!"

Tom, who was working a little distance from him, gasped, his face paling. "Are you sure?"

"Not really, but we can't ignore it. It could be one, and by the sound of so much ticking, it could be about to go off!"

"Oh, hell!"

Wilfred heard Tom's footsteps receding.

Second later, another face, that of their foreman, Mr Gooding looked down at Wilfred. "I've sent for help, the Bomb Disposal Officer will be here soon. Don't move an inch. That bomb could be sensitive. Any sudden movement by you could set it off."

Wilfred shivered at this.

Some time, later the Bomb Disposal Officer appeared. He climbed down gingerly. He whistled. "It's a whopper, 4,000 lbs, I reckon. All the people in this area – 20,000 – have been taken to safety. So if the bomb goes off, only you and I will be killed."

A great comfort, thought Wilfred, as he watched the Bomb Disposal Officer closely as he worked on the bomb. Time passed, how much exactly, he wasn't certain. A distant church clock had chimed the hour twice. So it must be two hours, but to him, with the nervous state he was in, it felt like double that. Would the bomb suddenly go off, blow both himself and the Bomb Disposal officer to Kingdom Come? He began to pray under his breath. He didn't want to die. He was too young to die. He had made so many plans for after the war, one of them was to start his own plumbing business. At last, he heard a soft click and the bomb stopped ticking. "That's done it!"

He began to breathe again.

Waving a cheery goodbye, the Bomb Disposal officer climbed out of the pit.

With shaking hands, Wilfred continued to work on the broken water main. So he wouldn't die today, after all. He decided when he wrote his daily letter to his mother he'd not mention finding the buzz bomb. There was no need to worry her unnecessarily. And all was well, as ended well.

After this traumatic experience, the passing days were uneventful – no more unexploded bombs turning up. He did his work, and in the evening, with Tom, Harry and Jack, enjoyed visits to the Windmill, as well as, at the cinema,; the latest films from Hollywood.

CHAPTER FOURTEEN

At the camp, Belinda's friend, Gillian, and her husband, Jimmy, was once more visiting them. The two women were chatting in the kitchen as they washed up the tea things.

Roger rose to his feet. "Would you like a beer?" he asked Jimmy. He was pleased to have got to know Jimmy, as he still missed his old pal, Charlie who had been transferred to another camp after they'd returned from America, though he still received a letter from him from time to time.

"I'll not say 'no'," Jimmy replied.

Roger nodded and went out of the room to the walk-in pantry in the passage which was adjacent to the kitchen. He took a pint bottle of Stout from off the marble shelf and was just returning to Jimmy in their living room when he heard Belinda mention his name. He stopped to listen. She was telling Gillian all about how, when they were at last in Oxford at his parents' she had accused young Alec of making a pass at her.

He heard Gillian gasp. "He didn't, did he? How awful! Fancy trying it on with his own brother's wife. Though, I suppose that sort of thing can happen at any time anywhere."

Belinda laughed. "I suppose it can, but it didn't really, not in this case." She explained to her what had happened on the stairs that morning. "I'm sure Alec had no ulterior motive when he pulled up the hem of my housecoat. He's not the sort, not like more than one fellow I've known in the past, but I just took the opportunity to use what had occurred to hopefully turn Roger against his family. I shouldn't have done it, I know, but I was desperate. You see he seems to be getting cold feet about leaving the UK once the war is over and returning to America. At one time he was really keen, couldn't wait to work on my dad's farm, but lately, I can tell he's having second thoughts. I want to go home. I've been away long enough. I can't bear the idea of not seeing Mom and Pop and all the rest of the family ever again, or at least not for many years.

Roger's fingers tightened on the neck of the beer bottle and he wished it was Belinda's neck. Fancy causing such an upset on purpose. What a sneaky little madam. He'd not have thought it of her, but it just went to show that you never really knew anyone else – even a wife whom you were supposed to be close to. He decided to have it out with her once Jimmy and Gillian had gone home.

After a game of cards and a few more beers, they said goodnight to Gillian and Jimmy, and Roger closed the front door. He turned. "Now," he said, "I've got a bone to pick with you."

Belinda frowned. "Bone! What do you mean? It's a phrase I've not come across before."

"You must have," retorted Roger. "You've been here long enough. Don't pretend you don't know what I mean. I overheard you talking to Gillian when the two of you were washing up; telling her about that row at Mum and Dad's the last time we were there. I know now that you just used that business with young Alec to try to turn me against my family, despite the fact you didn't really believe he'd tried it on with you. So what do you say about that?"

She swallowed hard. "You must have misheard me."

Roger's lips tightened. "You deny that you told Gillian about the incident and how you used it for your own ends."

"I had the faucet, I mean tap running. You must have got what I said all wrong."

"All wrong! Tap running! Don't give me that excuse. I'm not deaf you know, or daft! Admit that you're a conniving little madam. "

"I'm not."

"You're a bloody little liar, that's what you are, though." He stormed back into the living room, threw himself into his armchair and put on the wireless, turning the knob as far as it would go. Sound reverberated around the room. She put her hands over her ears. "It's too loud!"

He ignored her.

He ignored her too when she tried to make conversation with him over a deafening orchestral concert. And even when they were in bed, he purposely turned his back on her and pretended to be asleep. Before he drifted off, his thoughts turned to Susan, she'd never have behaved like Belinda had done. Caused such trouble!

* * *

They were back in Oxford once more, and Belinda and Roger had decided to go for a walk along the Botley Road to help to digest his mother's Sunday dinner. Suddenly, on the opposite side of the road, they saw Susan pushing a pram. Belinda recognised her from the wedding photograph that took pride of place on the wall of Mr and Mrs Bowler's passage. Then she noticed Roger's expression - it is obvious that he was thinking that the baby could have been his. Seeing this, the fact that she would probably never become a mother, sickened her more than usual.

Just after this, Hank had come from Didcot once more to meet up with her. She was extremely pleased to see him again, especially as no matter how much she tried there had been very little improvement in the state of affairs between her and Roger. When he wasn't on 'ops, he was in the Mess with his mates, drinking more, she imagined, than was good for him. There could have been other girls, too. She didn't know this for certain, but by the way he flirted with every female that he met up with, it was more than likely.

Seated opposite Hank in the Servicemen's club, she studied the face that was increasingly becoming dear to her. The relationship between them, apart from a kiss or two, was still platonic, although she knew it wouldn't take too much to alter that, on his side anyway. But even with the increasing gulf between her and Roger, she couldn't quite forget her childhood teaching at Chapel, that it was wrong to commit adultery. Not only that, but despite all his faults, she still loved Roger.

* * *

Roger, meanwhile, as Belinda had disappeared off somewhere without telling him where, as she often did, had decided to go for a drink in the Olde Gate Public House, which was near the station. Though he knew it wouldn't be the same drinking on his own. He recalled the recent letter he had received from his old mate, Charlie. If only Charlie could be with him at this very moment. They could have had a game of darts together. To his surprise, in the letter, Charlie had mentioned the little WAAF, Daisy to whom he had told a tall story to on Roger's behalf. Charlie, had run into her in the Mess at the camp he was now stationed at, and pointing her out had been told by one of his new mates, that it was no good making a play for her. It was common knowledge that she had lost her fiancé in an 'op over Germany, and since then, had refused to look at another man.

Roger had shrugged at reading about this in Charlie's letter – more fool Daisy to believe the lie about him. He entered the Public Bar, and to his astonishment whom should he see someone else he hadn't met up with for some time, his old friend, Lionel. Lionel had been at Grammar School with Roger and was also on leave. They clapped each other on the back.

"Fancy bumping into you," said Lionel.

"Fancy bumping into you, Lionel. How long is it since we last met?"

"A year, perhaps. How is life treating you? Pint, isn't it?"

"Yes, but I'll get these. "

"Okay. Thanks."

After getting their drinks, they seated themselves at one of the circular tables and brought each other up to date with what had happened in their lives since their last meeting.

"So how's Susan, are you married yet?" asked Lionel.

Roger looked rather shamefaced. "Not to Susan. I'm married to Belinda, an American girl."

Lionel whistled. "An American! Well, I never. How did that come about?"

"I was sent to train as a pilot in America, Alabama, in fact. "

Lionel took a satisfying slurp of beer and swallowed. "Well, that's a turn up for the book, I was sent to Alabama to train as a pilot, too.

"So are you a pilot now?" asked Roger.

"I am," replied Lionel with some satisfaction, wiping froth with the back of his hand from his handlebar moustache. "How about you?"

"Unfortunately, no. The 'Powers-that-be' decided that I wasn't fit enough to be one. It's a long story. I was rushed into hospital with appendicitis, I'd had a grumbling one for years. While I was there I met this nurse-aid. We fell in love with each other, and a few weeks later; me and Belinda were married."

'"That was quick. Was she...?"

"No, she wasn't! With the war on, we both decided we mightn't have time to waste."

"That's true. So what happened to Susan? I suppose you sent her a Dear-John letter?"

"Well, I had to, didn't I. Anyway, she's happily married now to a fireman and has recently had a baby."

"So all's well that ends well. So has there been a pattering of tiny feet for you and your Belinda?"

"Err, well, no. We've decided to leave having a family to after the war," Roger answered hurriedly; immediately changing the subject. "So how about you, are you engaged or married yet?"

Lionel laughed. "Not me. I like to play the field. I might marry later on if I survive this wretched war – perhaps, when I'm about forty. "

"So you've decided to sew all your wild oats first?"

"Too true."

"If you're not doing anything this morning, why don't you come down to see Mum and Dad, they'd be pleased to see you, I'm sure."

"Will your wife be there? I'd like to meet her?"

Roger almost choked on his beer. Would she be there? Half the time, when they came home on leave, he didn't know where she was. He knew what she told him; that she was meeting up with this woman friend whom she'd worked with at the Servicemen's Club, but was she? Of late, things hadn't been too good between them. It had not helped when he had tackled her about what he'd overheard that evening when her friend, Gillian and her husband, Jimmy came to tea.

"I'm sure Belinda would like to meet you, but she could be out shopping."

They had made their way to Bridge Street, and as Roger had foretold, his parents were delighted to see Lionel once more and hear all his latest news. He even stopped and shared their midday meal with them, one of Roger's mother's famous stews which she made with ham bones and vegetables from Roger's dad's allotment. Just as they'd finished the meal and his father had left to walk the short distance back to the Railway Workshop for his afternoon shift, a rather flustered Belinda appeared, carrying a bulging shopping bag. She looked somewhat surprised to see a stranger in their living room.

"This is my wife, Belinda," said Roger, introducing her to Lionel.

He put out his hand. "Hello, Belinda, I'm Lionel. Trust old Roger to pick himself a good looker."

Shaking his hand, she preened at the compliment. "Hi, hon."

"Lionel's my old school friend," Roger explained. "He went to train as a pilot in America too..."

"Though I never met a little dish while I was there like you," Lionel cut in.

Roger frowned. He didn't appreciate other men trying to flirt with his wife. "Anyway, Lionel made the grade, he is one now. He's on leave too. We just bumped into each other by accident. "

"That was a stroke of luck."

"It certainly was," said Lionel, glancing warmly at her.

Belinda and the two men spent the afternoon and evening together, playing darts, shove-ha'penny and cards. It was late when Lionel left to catch the last bus to the Cowley Swan and his parents' pub, The Swan.

CHAPTER FIFTEEN

Agatha Bowler was humming 'The White Cliffs of Dover' which she had heard Vera Lynn, the Forces Sweetheart, singing on the wireless, as she briskly swept the lino in the living room. Wilfred, her middle son was coming home – she glanced at the letter from him on the mantelpiece that had arrived the previous day. At least, with him back from London where he had been sent some months ago to repair the water mains damaged by the bombing, she could breathe easier. It was bad enough worrying about Roger being shot down by enemy aircraft, without the added concern of Wilfred. She only hoped this wretched war would be over before her Alec became old enough to be called up. She wondered when Wilfred would be arriving; he'd not said in his letter, but perhaps he didn't know for certain as yet. She bent and swept up the pile of debris into the dustpan. She heard the front door being opened, followed by footsteps. It was a bit early for the return of George from work, which was always just after midday.

"Mum!" called a familiar voice.

Her heart leapt. Wilfred! It was her Wilfred. The living room door flew open and her second son appeared in the doorway. She lay down the dustpan, threw her arms about him and pulled him to her, then reaching up, kissed his cheek soundly.

He pulled away. "Mum!"

She laughed. "I bet you'd not object to a kiss if I was a pretty girl."

He blushed. "Oh, Mum!"

"Well, let's have a look at you. You've grown! A couple of inches, I reckon since I last saw you. You've filled out too, so they must have been feeding you properly despite the rationing."

"Maybe, but the cooking wasn't as good as yours, Mum."

"Soft soaper."

He laughed. "It's the truth." He patted his stomach. "What's for dinner, I'm starving!"

"You've certainly not changed as far as appetite goes, anyway. It's my stew, followed by rice pudding – good thing I did extra. Your dad will be so pleased to see you when he gets in." She glanced at the clock on the mantelpiece. "Good grief! And that won't be that long, it's almost 11.30."

"I'll be pleased to see him. It seems I've been away for ages. How's our kid doing with the Electric Light Works, and has he got a girlfriend yet?"

"All right, I think with the Electric Light Works. Alec doesn't say much about it. It's a pity he couldn't get an apprenticeship like you did. He wanted to be a carpenter, you know, but with the war they weren't taking on apprentices. And as for a girlfriend, he keeps that close to his chest. Anyway, have you met anyone special while you've been in London?"

"One or two, no one serious."

She nodded. "Perhaps it's just as well. You're too young as yet. Anyway, I'd best lay the table."

Wilfred nodded. "And I'd better get unpacked."

* * *

As Wilfred put his clothing into the chest of drawers that he and Alec shared, he looked at the double bed that they also shared. How wonderful to get a decent night's sleep for a change. It was far from comfortable sleeping on the platform or on the stairs in the Underground. It hadn't been safe to stay in their digs though and far from pleasant to be woken by the house shaking and the loud explosions which seemed to get nearer and nearer. He came downstairs as the front door opened and his dad appeared. His father's face brightened and he smiled widely and gave Wilfred a bear-hug. "Hello, Son, Great to see you!"

Wilfred disentangled himself. "And you too, Dad."

They went into the living room and Agatha Bowler

dished up her stew, followed by a rice pudding cooked in the range's side oven.

George Bowler put down his spoon. "That was good, Mother." He turned to Wilfred. "So have you anything planned for tonight, Son?"

"Not really, why?"

"It's my evening for the Democrat Club. Will you come with me and your mother for a drink?"

Wilfred guessed his dad wanted to show him off to his mates. "Why not."

George Bowler smiled with satisfaction. "That's arranged then. "

That evening, they went to the Democrat Club which was just round the corner in South Street. The place was packed, the atmosphere, both noisy and smoky – most of the men were smoking cigarettes or pipes, though not all the women smoked. George and Wilfred had pints, while Agatha had a port-and-lemon. The two men played a couple of games of darts with some of George's workmates.

Wilfred won both games.

"You've improved since we last played darts," said his father ruefully.

"You've just become rusty, that's what it is," laughed Wilfred. "Old age catching up with you."

"Cheeky young whippersnapper, I'm only fifty, I'll have you know."

* * *

The weeks passed. Agatha was pleased that Wilfred seemed to have settled back down at his old job in Oxford. Then one Saturday evening they heard him washing himself in the sink in the scullery. He came into the living room where she and George were seated around the fire and listening to 'In Town Tonight' on the wireless. "I may be late back, Mum, Dad, don't wait up for me," he said.

"Where are you off to, Son?" she queried.

"Out!"

She turned to exchange a glance with George. Her expression saying, he's wearing his Sunday suit, and his hair is flattened down with water. Not only that, he's been out somewhere most evenings this week?

They heard the front door close.

"Reckon he's got a girl," said George with a chuckle.

Agatha frowned. "Do you think so?"

"It's what you've got to expect – he is twenty. I was courting the girls by the time I was twenty."

"I suppose you're right. It only seems like yesterday since he was in short trousers. I wonder if it's serious. If it is, I hope she's a nice respectable girl. And not a foreigner," she added wryly.

"That's not very likely, Wilfred's not been abroad to meet one."

A few days later, they learnt that he had indeed found himself a young lady when he asked if he could bring her to afternoon tea the following Sunday.

* * *

Agatha had been baking all morning – her celebrated small fairy cakes which she arranged on a paper doily on top of a glass cake stand. Next to this, on her best linen tablecloth was two large platefuls of egg-and-cress sandwiches, plus a plate of her home-made sausage rolls. At last, she and George heard Wilfred's voice in the passage, as well as an unfamiliar female voice. "They're here!" she exclaimed.

The living room door opened and Wilfred, along with a young woman with fuzzy dark hair entered, she was followed by a chubby little girl also with dark hair of around three.

"This is Janet," said Wilfred, indicating the woman, "Janet Thompson."

Smiling, she put out her hand. "Pleased to meet you, Mrs Bowler. And you, too, Mr. Bowler."

Forcing a smile, Agatha said, "Pleased to meet you."

She shook Janet's hand. Who was the child? And more importantly, whose child was she? Surely, she wasn't this Janet's? She couldn't be, could she?

George took his lead from Agatha and also shook Janet's hand.

Janet turned to the child. "Say hello to Mr and Mrs Bowler, Maureen," she urged.

The child threw her arms around Janet's legs and buried her head in Janet's skirt.

She disentangled herself from the small grasping hands. "She's shy," she said to Agatha. She turned to the child. "Now come on, Maureen, say hello, be a good girl for Mummy. "

Agatha gasped. Mummy!

"Hello," whispered Maureen.

"Hello, Maureen." She turned to Janet. "So who's this?"

"She's my daughter," replied Janet, somewhat defiantly.

"Your daughter!"

"Yes."

"I see."

They seated themselves at the table and Agatha poured the tea and passed it around, followed by the plates of sandwiches and sausage rolls. They began to eat. She swallowed her last mouthful of sandwich. She turned to their visitor. "So have you been married, Janet? Is your husband dead? Killed in this dreadful war, perhaps?"

"No," put in Wilfred. "Janet's not been married."

"Never been married! You mean she's had a child out of wedlock."

"Wedlock! How old fashioned can you be. This is the 1940's not the 1840's. I don't care if Janet's already got a child. She was let down. A married man took advantage of her. He let her think he was single," said Wilfred.

Agatha frowned. Was this true? Even if it was, she should have said 'no' to his advances. She must be a bad lot. If she hadn't have been she would have known 'right' from 'wrong'. "So how did you come to meet Wilfred?"

"Janet's a housekeeper for an old couple in Headington," put in Wilfred. "I was sent to their house on a plumbing job some weeks ago. Janet's friend has been minding Maureen of an evening so that we could see each other."

Agatha exchanged a look with George. So that's where he had been going of an evening all dressed up. She eyed Janet. Why couldn't he have got someone younger? Why, she must be at least five years older than him. Apart from age, someone without any encumbrances! Still, perhaps this wasn't serious, she consoled herself. Until Wilfred swallowed and said, "We want to get married."

"What! Married!"

"Yes, I love Janet and she loves me."

Marriage! Love! This was a nightmare! She'd wanted her boys to all marry nice respectable girls. She thought of her daughter-in-law, and not just respectable but ENGLISH. "That's as maybe, Wilfred, but all this is very hasty. You've not known each other all that long. Besides you're far too young. You're only twenty. You're not even getting your full wages as yet."

"I'll be twenty-one next birthday. And I will get my full pay then," replied Wilfred belligerently.

"Cool down, Son." George hesitated. "Look, leave it for a few months, at least. Get to know each other better. It's best not to rush into things; your mother and I had known each other for two years before we got married."

"Can't! Sorry, Dad, Mum, but Janet's expecting. I'm going to be a father. So will you give me your permission?"

Agatha choked on a mouthful of tea. "What!" This tart must have seduced her son, she was sure of it. Her boy knew right from wrong, she had seen to that. All her boys had been sent to the Baptist chapel every Sunday without fail. They all knew the Ten Commandments. Knew that sex before marriage was a sin.

"We'll have to think about it," said George.

After this bombshell had been dropped, she lost her appetite. She was right, this Janet was a trollop. How could they stop Wilfred from making the biggest mistake of his life? There must be some way. But what?

* * *

After Wilfred and Janet had taken little Maureen home, she and George discussed the matter.

"I'll write to Roger," said Agatha, "see what he has to say about all this. He and Belinda are here again next week. We should have a family discussion about Wilfred and this woman. Roger might have some idea how we can deal with the problem."

George agreed. Anything for a quiet life. But what they could really do about it, he didn't know. The damage was already done.

That night, Agatha couldn't sleep. Was this Janet just using her Wilfred as a meal ticket for herself and her bastard, she having already been pregnant once before, she couldn't have the excuse that she hadn't known what she was doing, and if they did marry, she mightn't be a faithful wife to Wilfred, he might never really know if the children he was bringing up were really his! Another idea struck her, what if this baby wasn't Wilfred's? After all, if she was so free with her favours, as she seemed to be, the expected child could be anyone's.

Some days later, things were made worse when worried out of her mind, she mentioned her problem to Ruth, a close friend of hers at the Baptist chapel, and the fact that Janet Thompson's family lived in Abingdon. Coincidentally, it turned out that Ruth's sister also lived there, unbelievably, next door to the Thompson's. According to Ruth the whole family had a very bad reputation. It appeared that Janet's grandmother, mother and several of her aunts had all had babies without the sniff of a husband!

One evening, a week later, when Wilfred had again dashed off to meet Janet, they were all seated around the table with a milk jug, cups and a pot of tea in front of them. All except Alec whom Agatha considered too young to hear them airing such an intimate problem. They had waited until Alec had left the house to go to the pictures.

She poured the tea and passed the cups around. "What should we do, Roger? How can we stop him? I think Wilfred is heading for a lot of trouble with this woman."

He frowned. "It's a tough one, Mum, but if you can talk him into giving her up despite her being pregnant, he could just pay her so much a week for the child's upkeep once it arrives. A few fellows at my camp realising they have made a mistake and no longer want to marry their former girlfriend have done that. "

"I don't think Wilfred would agree with such a thing," put in his father.

Agatha frowned. "Probably not!"

"I've seen the way he looks at Janet, he is really besotted," put in Belinda.

"But is she besotted with him, or is she just using him as a meal ticket?"

"We can't really be certain of that, Mum," said Roger.

"Wilfred's probably looking forward to being a father, Mrs Bowler. I wouldn't want to part with my baby if I was him," said Belinda wistfully.

"Well, no, I suppose not."

"Look," said George, "if we don't allow him to marry, we can only stop him for a short while as in just over a year he'll be twenty-one anyway and will be able to do as he pleases."

"That's true, and our refusal to accept this girl could turn him against us. We don't want a rift in the family. It's probably better to let him go ahead and marry this Janet even if we're not too happy about it, and just hope she'll turn out better than we think she will. I suppose she could turn out to be an ideal wife and mother. Though with her background, it's doubtful."

"We don't really know that," said George. "I say we let him go ahead and marry the girl. Is everyone agreed?"

Both Roger and Belinda nodded.

"What do you say, Mother?"

"I suppose so, George, I can't say I really like it, and if it turns out for the worse as I'm sure it will, let it be on your head!"

* * *

The banns were called at the Abingdon St Nicolas church in Abingdon, and three weeks later, on a rather dull Saturday afternoon, Agatha, very reluctantly; accompanied by George and Alec, attended the wedding. Wilfred, she knew would have had Roger as his best man, but unfortunately he couldn't get leave at that particular time so he and Belinda were unable to be present. Though Alec, togged up in his Sunday suit was quite proud to play that role.

The church itself, stone-built and hundreds of years old, lay amidst an ancient graveyard, the tombstones of which were mostly leaning and indecipherable; was packed out with Janet's relatives. Agatha, looking around wondered how many of them were illegitimate and so not quite respectable. Organ music played, and Janet obviously wearing a borrowed dress as it was too big for her, came down the aisle on the arm of some 'uncle' to where Wilfred, looking quite nervous was waiting in front of the altar. They said their vows to each other.

At this, Agatha blew her nose and wiped her eyes. Her poor boy, she had no faith that the marriage would turn out well.

After a lavish Wedding Breakfast, despite rationing; provided by Janet's family (had several 'uncles' given their rations up for the meal?) and which took place in their front room, the bride and groom, accompanied by Agatha, George and Alec returned to Oxford, where she had rented them a room with the use of the kitchen in an elderly woman's house on the opposite side to where they lived in Bridge Street.

Wilfred and Janet, saying 'goodnight' as soon as they could decently do so, disappeared off to their lodgings. But in the middle of the night Agatha was woken by an urgent knocking. She nudged George. "Wake up! There's someone knocking at our front door. You'd best go down and see."

"Must I?"

"Yes, you must."

Grumbling under his breath, George hurriedly got out of bed and went downstairs, pulling his overcoat off the peg in the passage and shrugging it on over his nightshirt. He unlocked the door and opened it to reveal a distraught half-dressed, Wilfred, and with him his equally half-dressed, almost hysterical new daughter-in-law.

"What's wrong?" he asked. "What are you two doing here at this time of night?"

Janet gulped, "Bedbugs!"

"What?"

She pulled back the sleeve of a hastily donned cardigan and scratched at her arm. "I'm bit all over. The bed in the room you fixed us up with in Mrs Ford's is riddled with those horrid little brown things. There was bloodstains on the sheets as well as their shed skins. Ugh! It makes me shiver just to think of them."

"Is this true?" asked Agatha, who had appeared, with a bed jacket over her nightdress behind him.

"Of course it is." snorted Janet. "Really, Mrs Bowler., why should I lie?"

"I suppose not, still I can't understand it. I know for a fact that Mrs Ford scrubs her front step every morning, and is very particular when it comes to keeping her house clean. I wouldn't have arranged for you to lodge there if I'd thought otherwise."

Janet looked disbelievingly at her mother-in-law. "Huh!" she said.

Agatha frowned. It was obvious that this Janet possibly did think that she might have arranged for them to lodge somewhere unsavoury on purpose. She didn't care for Wilfred's choice of wife but she would never do something like that.

"Maybe the bedbugs were brought in by a previous lodger?" suggested George.

"Could be that I suppose. Of course, I've never had them myself but I know all about them. They are small, flat wingless insects, the size and shape of an apple seed and feed on blood. They do not fly or jump but they can crawl rapidly. They hide during the day on beds, mattress seams, box springs, bed frames and headboards and come out at night. What did Mrs Ford have to say about all this? I gather you have told her."

"Yes, of course we have, and she wasn't too pleased to be woken up and be seen with her hair in curlers. Or to be told about the bedbugs – especially to hear about the bedbugs. She said it might have been her last lodger who had brought them in. She'd had her doubts about him as he was a bit scruffy looking. He went off owing her rent money."

"She shouldn't have taken him in if he was scruffy looking. It was asking for trouble."

Janet glared at her mother-in-law. "Well, she did, and it's us, me and Wilfred who have got to suffer for it."

Wilfred nodded. "Yes, Mrs Ford has told me that the mattress will have to be burnt and she expects me to do it for her in the backyard when I get back from work tomorrow evening."

"And you can go there on your own to do it, too," insisted Janet. "And when you've done that Wilfred you can fetch our belongings from there. I'm not going back into that house ever again."

Agatha pulled the front door open wider. "We'll have to talk about that. You'd best come in for now and I'll make us all a hot drink." As Wilfred and Janet followed her along the passage she thought, and where does this women imagine they are going to go to. I'm not having them here. I've got to keep the spare room free for when my Roger and the Yankee come home on leave. Besides they have left quite a few personal belongings in it. It just wouldn't be fair to put someone else in the room and chance whether or not they might go through them.

She put the kettle on and when it had boiled, made a pot of tea. Watching them drinking she decided that the best thing to sort out this latest problem was for George to spend the night, what was left of it, on the settee in the front room, while Wilfred could share again with Alec and she could share with Janet. For a moment she felt a bit guilty. It wasn't much of a honeymoon for newly-weds to have to sleep separately – though they had put the cart before the horse so to speak – their baby was due in five months. All the same, all this wasn't her fault. So why should she feel guilty?

* * *

After an uncomfortable couple of weeks, Agatha, much to her relief managed to find them some suitable accommodation to rent. This came about when she had a word with her landlord about her son and his wife and the problem they were causing her. He fortunately had a vacant bungalow to rent in Sunningwell, just outside of Abingdon. This bungalow had something that her house hadn't, an inside lavatory and a bathroom. She supposed this might make life easier for the tenants, but as she had never had such amenities, she didn't really see the need for them – a tin bath brought in from the shed was good enough for her; especially as with having such things, the rent would no doubt be dearer!

CHAPTER SIXTEEN

It was 1945 and May the 8th - V.E Day, and with Germany surrendering, at last the war in Europe which had dragged on for six years was over. Agatha, having heard the news on the wireless that morning was overjoyed. No more death and destruction, no more shortages, no more standing in queues, no more ration books. Though the war in the Far East with Japan still dragged on. She recalled the dazed state Roger had been in on more than one occasion when he'd come home on leave. He would sit with Tiger on his lap and stroke him in such a way that it was a wonder that the cat wasn't bald! It had almost broken her heart to see Roger's distress. Thank God, with the war ending that would be the end of that! And the end of the war wasn't the only thing she had to celebrate, she was now a grandmother. Her first grandchild, Ralph had been born a few days earlier to her son, Wilfred and his wife, Janet. She couldn't help but be excited at the news, even though she was still somewhat concerned at Wilfred's choice of wife. Also she still rankled at the carelessness of Janet when she'd asked her to feed the chickens for her when she and Wilfred were stopping with them and she had left the chicken run gate open and one of the chickens had got out. Both she and Janet had hunted high and low for it but never found it. She'd let Janet know in no uncertain terms how annoyed she was at this. She guessed one of her neighbours must have enjoyed a tasty chicken dinner.

The day before, she and George had been over to Sunningwell on the bus from Gloucester Green to see the new baby and taking with them as a gift, a rattle she had bought from Woolworth's, the famous 3d and 6d store in Cornmarket. She had nursed the new baby, and decided that little Ralph was delightful and the image of her Wilfred at the same age.

But now with the war having ended, she supposed that

her Roger might be carrying out his long held plan to emigrate to America. She was far from happy about this. If he should go such a distance away she probably wouldn't ever see him again. Though she supposed it was only natural that her American daughter-in-law, might miss her parents and long to be reunited with them. But if Roger and Belinda should settle in America, neither she and George, or Roger himself if he ever wanted to come home for a visit, were ever likely to have the kind of money to take such a lengthy sea voyage. She'd been told that it was a week to New York, and after that there would be a long train or bus trip to their ultimate destination. Besides, even if she and George could scrape the fare together which was extremely unlikely, she'd never been on a ship and mightn't be a good sailor. She didn't fancy being seasick and throwing up everywhere.

But while she was worrying about Roger and Belinda leaving England there was a falling out between her son and his wife. This was evidently caused by something that had been said to Roger by his friend, Lionel when both men, being on leave at the same time, had met up again. She couldn't help but overhear the row, the walls of the house between the bedrooms were thin and voices carried at night when everything was quiet, especially raised voices. She'd just dropped off to sleep when she was woken by Roger's angry voice. "So who is he then?"

"Who is who, hon?"

"That G.I. that Lionel has seen you with in the High Street, with his arms all round you. It's disgusting, canoodling with someone else, you're a married woman."

"What on earth is canoodling?"

"Don't act the innocent with me, you must know, kissing and cuddling."

Agatha frowned. Did he mean Hank, the G.I. that Belinda had brought home to their house a couple of times and who had generously presented her with food items that were impossible for her to get her hands on? But kissing, surely not, her daughter-in-law had told Agatha that she and Hank were just friends, and that he was lonely and far from home. With this dreadful war on her boys could be in the same position as Hank. If they were, she would be pleased if some other family should offer them the hand of friendship. But if that Yankee had lied to her, and that in truth it was more than friendship between her and Hank, well, if she'd have suspected that she would never have had him in the house.

"It was just a kiss on the cheek. In America friends kiss each other all the time. And put their arms about each other, we're not cold like you English. "

"Cold, cold, I'll give you cold, if you're lying to me, I'll...I'll..."

"Do what, Roger? Look, I'm not lying, Hank and I are just friends. Like you and some other ladies that you're pally with. Let me remind you that you're a married man, how do I know what you get up to with them?"

"I don't get up to anything with them."

"So you say. "

"It's true."

"Well, it's true about me and Hank only being friends."

"I bet he'd like more."

"Maybe so, but he's not getting it. Look, we've got to trust each other. If I say we're only friends then that's all we are."

"Whether you are just friends or not, I'd rather you didn't see him again, or get letters from him either."

"Huh! I'd rather you didn't chat up other women, but I don't suppose that you'll_stop doing that. Now, come on, give me a kiss and let's get some sleep."

"All right, then."

Agatha heard the sound of a brief kiss, followed by complaining springs as Roger and Belinda turned over in bed, then all went quiet.

Sighing, she turned over herself and closed her eyes, but try as she might she couldn't drop off as all her family's problems kept running through her head. Alec, so far hadn't caused any trouble to her and George, but for how long would that continue? She glanced at their alarm clock. Despite it being almost 11pm he still wasn't home. At the moment, she guessed he was joining in with the celebrations to mark the end of the war at Carfax, the centre of Town. What if, while he was there he should make the acquaintance of an unsuitable girl – one perhaps from Rosehill, the council estate at Rosehill had a bad reputation as regards an unruly element. A lot of the inhabitants having been moved out as part of slum clearance from St Ebbes in the centre of the town.

* * *

The streets of Oxford, George Street, Queen Street and Cornmarket were packed with mainly young people. In their hands were small Union Jacks which they waved enthusiastically from time to time. In front of the Carfax Tower, from which, proudly fluttered a large Union Jack, a great crowd sang at the tops of their voices, as they danced around a huge bonfire, rejoicing that the war had at last ended and they could now look forward to a peaceful future. Alec, too, amidst the crowds was enjoying himself, he'd never before had so much success with the girls. He held the hand of one on each side of him. He'd lost count of how many girls he had actually kissed in the last few hours. He wondered whether he could pluck up enough courage to ask one of these girls if he could see her home.

He turned to the girl on his right hand side, a rather pretty redhead about the same age as himself. "Could I...?"

"What?" she queried, looking him up and down.

"Err, see you home," he stammered.

She smiled. "If you like, but I live quite a distance away – Rosehill Council Estate. And the last bus will have gone. I'm going to have to walk it."

"If you like I could walk home with you," he said.

"All right, then. I'll just tell my mates that you're taking me home." She moved over to some other girls and spoke to them. Eyeing him up and down, they giggled.

She returned. "So what's your name?" she asked.

"Alec. And you?"

"I'm Agnes."

They started to walk along the High Street, then over Magdalen Bridge, around the war memorial in the Plain where soldiers from WW1 were buried, and along the Iffley Road. They climbed the steep Rose Hill for which the area had been named. At last, they reached the council estate.. "I live in Ashers Way," she said. By this time, Alec had learnt that Agnes worked as a counter assistant in the Coop Drapery in George Street. They reached her house. Like all the houses in Oxford, the low railings around the gardens that had previously been there were missing, having been taken away for the war effort. Plucking up courage, after arranging a date with her for the following evening at the Regal Cinema in Magdalen Road, he bent his head to hers, then kissed her. He then had to walk all the way home, a distance of about three miles. In their living room his dad was waiting for him. He looked him up and down. "Have you been out with a girl?"

"I have, so what?"

"No decent girl would be out to this time. I'm off to bed."

Behind his dad's retreating back, Alec pulled a face. He'd felt like saying, 'How do you know I've been out with a DECENT girl?'

* * *

Over the next few weeks there seemed to be celebrations for the end of the war everywhere. There was a party in Bridge Street itself where all the hoarded foods – hoarded from 1939 were brought out and trestle tables covered in bed sheets in the middle of the street groaned with sandwiches, sausage rolls, pork pies and little cakes iced with red, white and blue icing to represent the Union Jack. There were dishes of jelly and blancmange, tin fruit and jugs of evaporated milk. All of which were washed down with beer for the adults and lemonade for the children. Even a piano was brought out from someone's house and lively tunes were played which people sang and danced to. They did a conga all along South Street, North Street and West Street, then back into Bridge Street, sticking out their legs and singing, "I...yi...I...yi, a conga, I...yi, I...yi, a conga..."

Alec, didn't attend the party as he considered he was far too old for such jollification, though, he watched the dancers from a distance. Not so, his parents, George and Agatha, they were in the thick of it, especially with the dancing of the conga. The party went on until late, all the windows with blackout curtains were drawn back and lights shone out everywhere.

* * *

After the cinema visit, Alec had met Agnes, the girl from Rosehill, a couple of times for a walk along the river bank – he'd even taken a punt out of one occasion. Then suddenly she stood him up. Why, he didn't really know, though it might have been, he thought later, because he had treated her with respect – keeping his hands to himself. Secretly, he was somewhat upset, but then he thought that his mother wouldn't have approved of Agnes as she was always saying that she hoped he wouldn't get tangled up with someone from Rosehill as she considered girls from that area of Oxford as being rather common. She certainly wouldn't have approved of the red nail varnish on Agnes' fingernails. And after all, at eighteen he had plenty of time to settle down, as there were a million other fish in the River Thames.

* * *

As the months passed he'd met one or two other girls, though after a couple of dates they always seemed to dump him. How he wished he was as handsome as Roger, and with the gift of the gab which Roger had in abundance. Then he would have had girls flocking. Still, he did dump one girl himself. To his surprise, this girl had actually asked him out. He'd met Gloria in a pub where he'd gone to play darts with a mate. The trouble was she was very fat. He felt embarrassed to be seen out with her. Then she gave him a rude poem – one with an explicit description of the sex act - not that he knew much about such things. This poem had the effect of turning him on, but he was also disgusted by it. And now with Belinda and Roger packing their trunks for America, he suddenly realised how much he was going to miss him when he was gone. The idea that he'd probably never see him again was difficult to take. Roger had promised he would send him the fare, once he was settled in himself, if he should decide to join him. He didn't think it likely that he'd ever want to leave England. He wasn't adventurous like Roger, and the thought of never seeing his parents, or even Wilfred again, gave him a hollow feeling.

* * *

One year later, June 1946. From a deckchair on the Queen Mary where he was seated, Roger admired the glittering wavelets that stretched as far as the eye could see until a pack of young kids appeared, the children of the scores of GI Brides on board. He hastily put his hands over his ears to try to deafen the noise that they were making, as shouting and squealing, they rampaged up and down the deck of the huge liner that he and Belinda were sailing to America on. Apart from the noisy children, the voyage had plenty to keep everyone amused, from knitting classes (not that he was interested) bingo nights, card tournaments, quizzes, hat-making contests, sing-alongs, classical concerts and ballroom dancing, though he had got into trouble with that when he'd asked one of the GI Brides to dance. Belinda had just gone off in a huff back to the cabin they were sharing because she'd observed him passing the time of day with another of them and accused him as usual of flirting with her. She refused to belief that he'd only been telling the girl that he was a G.I. Bridegroom as he'd married an American like she had, only a girl in his case. They were lucky to have a cabin to themselves, though. A cabin with twin beds and a porthole at one end. This was because they were husband and wife. The majority of the other passengers being GI Brides with children had to share – eight to a cabin with bunks placed one over the top of the other.

He looked down at himself, it still seemed strange to be wearing civvies instead of his uniform. Roger had at last been discharged from the R.A.F. He thought back to the row he and Belinda had had in bed that night, now several months previously when he'd tackled her about the Yank. After a heated argument, they'd made it up as they always did, and thinking they would have a better life in America than in England, and knowing what she really wanted, he was determined that they should leave for there as soon as possible.

When he'd made enquiries about this from the American authorities he been told that before leaving for the States he would have to be processed at Tidworth, a U.S. army camp outside Salisbury. When he'd arrived there he'd found the camp was full of G.I. Brides who were also to be processed. He certainly was outnumbered as he was the only G.I. Bridegroom there. He like the girls was given a medical, but unlike them he didn't need an internal examination with the aid of a torch.

He recalled the tears of his mother and the stiff upper lip of his father on the day of their departure from Oxford. Even his two brothers', Wilfred and Alec had looked somewhat shaken that the moment of his leaving England, possibly for ever, had actually come. That leave-taking had certainly caused him a pang or two, though he tried not to show it.

It couldn't be helped, he told himself; both he and Belinda had to think of themselves and their future.

Excitement filled him as he visualised the sunlit fields of his father-in-law's farm. With his strong young arms to do the work in half the time that the old fellow did and all the ideas he had to improve the farm's yield, he couldn't wait to get started.

* * *

Belinda, meanwhile was seated on one of the beds in their cabin. She thought of Hank, she always did, after she and Roger had had one of their rows, and that maybe, she would have been better off with him. She wondered if Hank had settled down okay back in his home town. He had left the U.K for the U.S. a few months earlier. She glanced through the porthole at the sea, today it was as still as a millpond, a brilliant blue, like the sky, with golden glints of sunshine edging the wavelets, but a couple of days back, with it being stormy weather it had been a dingy grey, with waves that had risen as high as mountains, before sinking back down again. Of course, she was seasick, and the sight of them had made her recall her time in the lifeboat and how terrified she had been, and last night she'd had a nightmare, her first for ages. She only hoped she wouldn't have another nightmare tonight. All the same, what a lot had happened to her since her ordeal in the lifeboat. Some good, some bad. And now, at last, she was going home. How she was looking forward to seeing Mom and Pop and the rest of the family. She rose, having decided to go and re-join Roger on deck before one of those wretched Limey's should lead him astray.

At last, the voyage was over and they arrived in St Johns, Newfoundland, after which she and Roger travelled by train and Greyhound bus to their destination and were reunited with her family. Tears of joy followed, instead, she imagined, tears of distress that his family had bravely tried to blink back at Oxford Railway Station.

CHAPTER SEVENTEEN

Agatha sighed with relief as she gingerly seated herself on a dining room chair. Both George and Alec had left for work and she'd somehow managed to wash up the breakfast things. She felt so ill and over the last few months it was getting worse the dragging sensation in the lower part of her tummy. She supposed she ought to go and see Dr Green, but what if she'd something really wrong with her and needed an operation? They'd not got the money to pay for something like that. She wondered if this National Health Service with its free medical treatment and glasses that George had read about to her from the Oxford Mail would actually happen. It seemed too good to be true. But apart from a free operation who would look after George and Alec while she was in hospital, and not only that, but after an operation, she might need to be looked after herself for some time. Best to keep quiet and put up with the discomfort.

She heard a knock on the front door and groaned. Who could that be? With difficulty she rose and made her way slowly along the passage. She hoped it wasn't a neighbour wanting to borrow a cup of sugar – she needed all their ration to make George's little fruit cakes.

She opened the front door. To her surprise she saw Janet with little Maureen beside her and baby Ralph in a pushchair.

"Hello, Mrs Bowler. I was coming in for the Cattle Market and I thought I'd call round and let you see the kids."

"That's good of you. You'd best come in."

Janet pushed the pushchair into the passage and indicated the sleeping Ralph. "I'll leave him where he is, he'll be okay. She turned to her mother-in-law. "How are you?" she asked.

Agatha closed the front door. "Not so bad", she replied. She made her way back to her living room, with Janet and little Maureen following her.

All of a sudden, she writhed in pain.

"What's the matter?" asked Janet, concern in her voice.

"Nothing," she muttered, entering the living room.

"Doesn't look like nothing to me."

"I'll be all right when I sit down." Agatha carefully seated herself on her chair. Despite her brave words, tears filled her eyes and she weakly began to cry.

Janet frowned. "There is something wrong with you. You can't deny it. How long have you been like this?"

There was no reply.

"My guess is months, rather than weeks. You need to see your doctor. "

"It's not necessary. " She pulled an already sodden handkerchief out of the pocket of her apron and blew her nose.

"Oh, yes, You need to contact him. What's his phone number."

"I don't know it," mumbled Agatha, wiping her eyes.

"The phone number will be on your medical card. Where do you keep it?"

"They're behind the vase on the mantelpiece."

Janet picked up the cards and studied them. "Ah, here's the number. I'll go to the shop over the road and get someone to phone your doctor. Get him to come and examine you. I won't be long." She left the house accompanied by the children and crossed the road to the grocery shop.

"What can I get you?" asked Mr Bird, the owner.

"Nothing, I'm afraid. This is an emergency. It's my mother-in-law, Mrs Bowler. She's taken poorly. Will you phone her doctor for me? His phone numbers on the medical card." She handed him the card and the tuppence for the call."

"Certainly." Mr Bird studied the medical card. "Dr Green, I know him. He's my doctor too."

Mr Bird rang Doctor Green's surgery and told him that one of his patient's, Mrs Bowler from Bridge Street had taken ill and would he visit her? Doctor Green looked up his patients' records and found her details. He promised to call.

This he did.

Dr Green asked Agatha some questions and examined her. "I think it's a retroverted womb."

"What's that?"

"In layman's terms, my dear, it's a dropped womb. You will need an operation. I will arrange for you to be admitted to the Radcliffe Infirmary as soon as possible."

She wasn't really surprised. For a long time now she'd needed to wear a cloth between her thighs to support something that protruded from her privates. But an operation. How would they pay for it? Perhaps if she sent an airmail letter to Roger and Belinda explaining the situation. Roger had earned good money while in the R.AF. Four times or more the amount his father earned. She didn't like to ask them for the money as they'd need all they had to set themselves up in America. But she'd no choice.

Before she went home Janet fetched her an airmail letter from Botley Road Post Office. Agatha wrote a few lines and Janet promised to post the letter on her way home to Sunningwell.

* * *

Roger turned off the engine of the John Deare Tractor and sighing he pulled off his peaked cap and wiped his sweating brow with his handkerchief. He was so hot. He wondered how long it would take him to get used to the heat of Alabama, especially when he was doing manual work? He had offered to plough a couple of Pop Jones' fields for him. Pop was to get a subsidy from the U.S. government to cultivate some acres that had been lying fallow for some time. The idea was that Pop plant a crop on them. He wondered if his father-in-law would actually do this? Whatever ideas he'd suggested that the older man could do to improve the farm's yield, had to date been ignored. Apart from this he found that life with the close proximity of so many of his wife's siblings rather trying. They were so lively and quite unlike their English counterparts. All four of them had at last left school. Jimbo was now studying in College, while Johnny helped his dad on the farm. The two girls, Brenda and Betsy, having blossomed into attractive young women since he had last seen them were both employed in offices as clerical assistants in a nearby town.

He climbed down from the tractor. Perhaps the reason for him feeling down was he was missing the RAF and all his mates, as well as the flying.

He had recently heard from his mother in England that she needed an operation. Seeing his mother's handwriting on the airmail he'd thought at first there was something wrong with his father. She didn't normally write to him, leaving the letter writing to his dad as she wasn't much of a writer. Her mother had died of cancer when she was nine and she'd not liked her father marrying again. Consequently, she'd played up her stepmother, and having left school at twelve, she 'd been sent into Service.

In her letter, she wouldn't say what exactly what was wrong with her, and puzzling it over with Belinda she suggested that the operation might be a hysterectomy. He knew that women of his mother's generation were very bashful when it came to discussing intimate problems so that very well could be the case. Evidently, Janet, Wilfred's wife had found her crying when she went to call in with the children, and had insisted she get the doctor to her. But the main problem was that the operation would have to be paid for as only his father was in the hospital club. He knew his parents didn't have much money. His dad's wage at the Railway Workshops was hardly generous. And though his mother didn't exactly ask him to pay the medical expenses for her, he knew that she hoped that he would.

Feeling he had no choice but to do this, he had gone to

his bank and arranged for a bank draft for a considerable sum to be sent to her immediately – he was thinking of buying a house of their own, and though the houses in Alabama were built of wood and not as dear as the brick-built houses in England, he still needed all the money he could scrape together to purchase one. With the money he had left in his bank account he would now need to buy a smaller house in a poorer neighbourhood.

* * *

Several weeks had passed. He'd heard from his mother that she had received the money which she thanked him very much for. He knew that by now she would have had her operation. He only hoped she had come through it all right. After all, she was fifty six and not getting any younger. How on earth would he feel if something should happen to her, and how would Dad and Alec manage without her? How were they managing at the moment? Dad could hardly do more than boil a kettle. How could he provide meals for himself and Alec, especially after being at work all day? With his mother around Dad wouldn't have been encouraged to do such things. The old fashioned idea was that the man went out to work at a paid job, and that the women saw to the children. and the shopping, and did everything else in the home. Though some who were desperately poor, had a sick husband perhaps, took in washing and ironing. Apart from his job the only thing a man was supposed to do was to see to any repairs in the house, and see to the garden. Or maybe an allotment like his dad.

He felt so helpless at being so far away in his parents' time of need. Something like this, that they might be ill had not occurred to him before.

* * *

Agatha had recovered from her operation and was about to

121

be discharged. While she'd been away, to her relief, her neighbour, Mrs Paxford, refusing to take anything for her trouble, had helped out by getting in shopping and sending in a hot meal for George and Alec every evening.

The doctor on his rounds approached her bed. "Now, Mrs Bowler, you do realise that you must take it easy for a couple of weeks," he insisted.

"Err, well, yes..."

"No rushing home to do housework and wait on your family. I think it best that you go into a convalescent home until you can get back on your feet."

She bit her lip. A convalescent home would cost money, which she and George didn't have. She couldn't ask Roger and Belinda for any more. What on earth could she do?

"Unless, of course you could be cared for by a relative." he added.

To her surprise, as well as George and Alec, she'd been visited by Wilfred accompanied by Janet. Later that day, at visiting time, they appeared again. She confided to them her problem.

"That's easy," said Janet. "You must come to us in Sunningwell so I can look after you."

Agatha's mouth dropped open. "What? But you've got two young children to look after, as well as Wilfred and yourself."

"That's as maybe, but you're family. I want to look after you, and I won't take no for an answer. "

To think she had got this girl all wrong. She couldn't be that bad to offer to do this. "That's very good of you."

Janet patted the older woman's arm. "Not at all. So that's settled then."

So after leaving the Radcliffe Infirmary, Agatha was taken by ambulance to Sunningwell where she was so well looked after that she soon returned to full health.

* * *

Belinda heard Roger's footsteps. The kitchen door, the window wire meshed to keep out the insects opened and he entered. She flipped over a French pancake that she was frying for their breakfast. She turned to see him holding a letter in his hand. "Oh, you've been down to the mail box, hon, anything interesting?"

He didn't reply. Then he purposely ripped up the letter in front of her and threw the pieces on to the floor. "I'll give you interesting," he growled. "It was from him! That Yank!"

"He's not a Yank, Yanks are from the North, he's a Southerner like me."

"If I say he's a Yank, then he's a Yank. You've been writing to him and after I told you not to!"

"Why shouldn't I write to Hank, we're only friends, you've got your female friends at the Gas Corporation, or is it one rule for men and another for women?" She hastily flipped over the pancake again. "Look what you've done with your jealousy, it's burnt!"

"I don't care if it is. I told you not to have anything to do with him."

"I can do as I please," she replied belligerently.

"You're my wife, mine, you should not be chasing after other men."

"I'm not!"

"Huh!" Furiously, he kicked at the leg of the table which she had laid up ready for breakfast and the pot of Maple syrup for the pancakes tipped over and toppled onto the floor; smashing, leaving broken shards of glass glittering in a stream of syrup.

"Look what you've done, you won't be able to have any syrup on your pancakes now."

"I don't want any. Don't want anything! I'm off to work." He turned on his heel and she heard the kitchen door bang-to behind him, and seconds later, his automobile start up. Sadly, she cleared up the mess. Things were not becoming any easier between her and Roger even though a few months previously they left the farm and moved into this three-bedroomed house with a cellar beneath it at Mount Olive. He'd also landed a reasonably paid clerical position at the Alabama Gas Corporation in Birmingham so money wasn't tight.

Later that morning after finishing her housework, she decided to make herself a coffee. She put coffee grounds into the percolator, turned on the faucet and added water to the pot. She had just sat down with her cup when she heard a knock at the door. She patted her hair. Who could that be? She wasn't expecting anyone. Of course, it could be the woman from next door. Isabel was twenty years her senior with grown children but she seemed quite friendly. And Belinda had invited her to come for a coffee whenever she had the time to spare.

She opened the door. To her astonishment, it wasn't Isabel at all. It was a widely smiling, Hank, holding a bunch of pink carnations. "Hank! What are you doing here?"

"I've come to see you, can I come in?"

She thought quickly, Roger wouldn't like it, but to hell with him. It was her house too, she'd ask in whom she liked. "Of course, you can, Hank. It's lovely to see you again." She opened the door wider.

He came in and handed her the carnations. "For me?"

"Of course, for you."

"She sniffed at them appreciatively. "How lovely! I'd best put them in water straight away." She found out a vase, filled it with water and arranged the flowers in it. She placed the vase on her windowsill and standing back admired them. "If Roger asks me where they've come from I'll say that Isabel took me to the store in Town and I got them there." She turned to Hank. "So how's life treating you since you got back to the States?

"Fine. I'm going back to my old job in Real Estate, they've kept it open for me."

"That's a coincidence. Roger, before he joined the RAF also used to sell houses. In England Real Estate is called an Estate Agents. His firm kept his job open for him too if he'd wanted it."

They chatted for a while, then they both saw a flash of lightning and heard a loud rumble of thunder. "Sounds like a storm's getting up," said Hank.

She shivered. "As long as it's not a tornado."

They both went outside onto the porch. The wind was indeed getting up. They could hardly keep their feet. Apprehensively, they studied the sky. There was a huge white cloud overhead that with the dirt and debris swirling around was quickly changing to black.

"I don't like it," frowned Hank.

Belinda hung onto the rail surrounding the porch for all she was worth. "Neither do I, I think we'd best go down to the cellar, in case it turns into a full blown tornado. It should be safer down there."

Hank agreed and followed her down the cellar steps. She struggled to open the trapdoor, but the wind, by now, was so strong, it almost wrenched it off its hinges. At last, they found themselves inside, and with both her and Hank together pushing-to the door, they somehow managed to close it.

Once they were inside the noise of the wind lessened, though it seemed to make the whole house shake on its foundations. She thought of the tornadoes she'd heard about – the worst one having a F5 wind speed of $261 - 318$ mph and strong enough to lift up an 83 ton train and toss it 80 feet from the tracks. Automobiles on the roads, too, became missiles as they flew through the air.

It was dark in the cellar, the electric light having flickered, then died. Seated on chairs left down there in case of need. Hank suddenly leant over and took both her hands in his. "I love you," he said, a tremor in his voice. "I know you're not happy with Roger. I know you've not said in so many words, but I can sense it. Why don't you leave him for me? I'd treat you right. You wouldn't want for anything."

"I know I wouldn't," she whispered in reply, "but I can't, you see I love Roger, whatever his faults, and he's got quite a few, I love him."

"I see," he replied sadly. "There's no more to be said, is there."

"I'm sorry." Suddenly, she slapped a hand across her mouth as she recalled her wedding photograph on top of her bureau that was turned over on its front. It always ended up like that whenever she and Roger had a row. "I must go back up into the house."

"Whatever for? It could be dangerous up there."

"I've left behind my most precious possession."

"What on earth is that?"

"My wedding photograph." She headed for the trapdoor and struggled with it. Seconds later she had the trapdoor open and was heading up the stairs almost losing her balance as she was buffeted by the wind.

He rushed after her. "Come back! You'll get yourself killed!"

They stood together on the shaking porch. The sky in front and above them was filled with swirling dust and dirt. Even garden implements, and an uprooted tree whirled past. At that moment there was a terrific bang, and the whole structure of the house shook violently, before blowing away, and taking them with it.

CHAPTER EIGHTEEN

Roger drove his automobile slowly along the street – what was left of it, hardly able to believe his eyes. Where were the houses? It looked like there'd been a bomb blast – there was wreckage everywhere, pieces of shattered wood and smashed tiles. So where had his house been? He couldn't tell. And where was his Belinda? Had she heard in time the warning on the wireless of an approaching tornado due to hit the Mount Olive area? Please God, she'd managed to get to safety. The weather warning had been picked up by someone at the Alabama Gas Corporation offices, and had gone round them with the speed of a forest fire. He had immediately left work and made his way home to Mount Olive.

Feeling so helpless, he decided to drive to the nearest Community Centre. He knew that in such terrible circumstances like this, people evacuating their homes might come there en-mass until the danger was passed. He neared the large brick built building, which unlike the wooden houses was able to stand the devastating winds. He'd heard about these tornadoes since living in the U.S. Evidently, thunderstorms likely to give birth to tornadoes were called super cells. Tornado winds were the fastest on earth. It could sometimes hop along its path destroying one house and leaving the one next door untouched. Not that this had happened in the street he was beginning to call home - the place had completely disappeared, apart from the rubble.

At the Community Centre he located the main entrance. He pushed open the door and went inside. The large room was packed with at least a hundred people, sitting or lying on mattresses on the floor. He saw a woman in a white nurses' uniform. Might she know something? He approached her. "Excuse me," he said. "I'm looking for my wife, Belinda Bowler. Has she been brought in here?

She looked surprised at hearing his English accent, but

soon recovered herself. "Come with me," she said moving towards a desk in the middle of the room, and consulted a clipboard. She ran her eye down the list of names. "Belinda Bowler, you say? "

"That's right."

"Sorry, there's no one here of that name."

Roger swallowed. He'd hope she'd be here, safe and sound. "Could she be somewhere else in the vicinity?"

The woman frowned. "Could be, I suppose. She could have taken shelter somewhere and turn up in a day or two. Your best bet is to consult the State Police who will let you know if they hear anything."

"Thank you," said Roger, for what he wasn't certain.

With dragging steps his throat tightening as if he had a rubber band around it, he left the Community Centre and returned to his vehicle. Where should he go now? The farm was the only place he could think of, and Pop and Mom Jones would have to know that their daughter was missing. He couldn't just tell them something like that over the phone.

The journey seemed to take forever. At last he reached the farm. They were surprised to see him, especially with him looking so haggard and dishevelled. "What's wrong?" asked Pop, noting Roger's expression.

"It's Belinda," he said shakily. "A tornado has struck Mount Olive, wrecking our street and house."

Pop's face whitened. "What!"

"Belinda!" cried Mom. "She's not with you."

"No."

"So where is she? Is she all right?"

"I don't know. She's missing," said Roger, hardly able to get the words out.

"Oh, no!"

Pop put his arms around Mom who was sobbing. "My little girl, where's my little girl."

Roger tried to pull himself together. "Can I phone the State Police, see if they have heard anything?"

"Sure can. And you can stay here with us as long as is

necessary."

* * *

A week or so later Roger did hear something. A female body of about Belinda's age and build had been recovered from a stream quite some distance from Mount Olive. The State Police sent for him to see if he could identify it.

The morgue attendant pulled back the sheet. "I'm afraid the body is rather bloated after being in the water for some time so it might not be that easy to recognise who it is."

Roger looked down at the waxen doll. Was this his wife? The hair was the same shade and length. The woman wore a wedding ring, a plain gold band like the one he had given Belinda, on the third finger of her left hand, so whoever she was, she'd been married. She even had a mole on the left hand side of her cheek exactly the same as Belinda.

"I'm not certain."

"Look again. Take your time."

He looked again. He didn't recognise the dress. But she was always buying new clothes and it could be a dress he'd not yet seen. Yes, that could be it.

He studied the body before him. It had to be her, didn't it?

He made up his mind. "Yes, that's my wife, Belinda Bowler."

The morgue attendant recovered the body and offered his condolences to Roger. He left the room, choking with tears that he refused to shed. He'd loved Belinda. All that business with Hank, just seemed so unimportant now.

* * *

Agatha, tears of joy running down her face, clutched the airmail letter to her bosom. He was coming home, her first born was coming home. She felt like singing at the news. She reread the letter, she couldn't believe her eyes,

Belinda, his wife, was dead. Dead! It didn't seem possible, but evidently it was true. She'd not been too keen on her it was true, but she didn't want her to be dead. She'd been caught in one of those terrible tornadoes that they often got out there in the States with winds so strong they could blow away whole houses and the occupants with them. In fact, this was what had happened to the house where she and Roger were living. Thank God that at least he had been at work at the time, and miles away. She was sorry the girl was dead at only 22. She was no age. She should have had all her life before her. It was a tragedy Still, the most important thing was that her boy was coming home. Hopefully, to never leave his family and Oxford again!

She hardly let George get in the door when he came for his meal at dinnertime when she told him the exciting news, gabbling in her haste to get the words out. Learning of his daughter-in-law's untimely death, he struggled to prevent his face from brightening. She knew he'd been missing Roger badly and in truth was as pleased as she was to learn that their eldest son would be returning soon. They had tried to tell themselves that they'd been lucky that he hadn't been killed in the war as so many other young men had been, even if now he was going to go thousands of miles away, but in reality this hadn't really made them feel any more accepting of the fact.

"I wonder if Rumble & Badstocks will let him have his old job back?" said Agatha.

George frowned. "It might be a bit too late for them to honour their promise as regards that, Mother."

"I suppose so."

He seated himself at the dining room table and Agatha dished them up portions of the stew she had made. They began to eat, but within minutes both of them had laid their spoons back down on the tablecloth, being too excited to eat. "Still, he's sure to find something else with all his experiences," said George.

"Yes, he might be able to find a managerial position at the Morris Motors Works at Cowley."

"That's true."

Within a few days, the tragedy, and the fact that Roger would soon be returning from the States had spread to all their friends and neighbours. When Janet had come in from Sunningwell on the bus for one of her visits with the children, Agatha couldn't wait to tell her the exciting news. The two women were now the best of friends, Janet's mother-in-law having warmed to her since she'd been looked after so well after her operation. She'd decided that Janet had a lot of good in her. When convalescing, nothing had been too much trouble for the girl, she only had to mention what she required for it to be done for her. She recalled the time when, she and Wilfred were stopping with them and she'd given the girl a good ticking off for letting out the chickens from their run after feeding them. She'd known the catch on the gate to the run was faulty. She now regretted how she had spoken to her. She knew now, too, that it had been foolish of her to listen to gossip about Janet's family. It had certainly taught her a lesson, that's for sure – she'd never listen to idle gossip about anyone ever again.

A few weeks later, Roger sailed into Liverpool, and then took a train to Oxford. Before his arrival, Agatha had brought out the red, white and blue bunting that they'd had up for the street party at the end of the war, and Alec had strung it up in Bridge Street, criss-crossed from the houses on the one side of the street to those on the opposite side.

The whole family, and some of the neighbours too, met Roger when he arrived at Oxford Station. As the train steamed in and with a screech finally slowed to a halt, loud cheers filled the air. These were followed by tears, hugs and kisses. One of Oxford's sons had returned!

That evening, George, accompanied by Agatha had taken Roger and Alec to the Democrat Club where all the members there, to welcome him back, had shook his hand, and Roger never needed to buy a single drink all evening.

CHAPTER NINETEEN

The days, followed by the weeks, passed. Although he missed Belinda desperately, he wasn't sorry to be back amongst his own people. Gradually as the year 1946 had changed to 1947, he'd begun to feel unsettled in America – despite there being so many luxury goods that could be obtained in the States, goods that were unheard of in the U.K., it just wasn't home. And after such a tragedy of losing Belinda, he wanted to go home.

He had been up to his old firm, Rumble & Badstocks and they had willingly taken him back on. He'd also been fishing several times with Lionel. Having tried both sea fishing and river fishing, he'd decided he preferred the river fishing to the sea fishing from the pier in Gulf Shores. Lionel was now running a little newsagent and sweet shop in Between Town's Road, Cowley, his parents, as a welcome home present having bought the leasehold for him.

There was rather a cool atmosphere as regards himself when, as they usually did, Susan's parents came to play cards with his mum and dad. But he supposed that was only to be expected after the way he had treated their daughter. Mrs. Swift kept telling him how happy their Susan was with her husband, that he would do anything for her, and that their little boy, John, now three years old, was delightful.

He supposed he should be pleased that Susan was happy. He felt guilty sometimes at the way he had treated her in the past. But the past was the past, it was too late now to ever make amends.

* * *

It was a few weeks since Susan had heard that her former fiancé, Roger had returned to Oxford. She smiled across at her little boy who was playing with some toy soldiers in his playpen. She put him in that when she was busy as left free to roam he'd been into all manner of mischief. But that she supposed was young children for you.

She ran her hot iron over a pillowcase and added it to the pile of clean washing. There was a knock on the door. She replaced the iron onto the ironing board. She eyed the child. "Now, who can that be, John?" she said.

His eyes brightened, and he licked his lips. "Grandma with some sweeties for John," he answered, hopefully.

She opened the front door. To her surprise, it was one of her husband's colleagues. "Hello Pete," she said. "What brings you here?"

Then she noticed the way he could hardly look her in the eye. She felt a cold sensation in the pit of her stomach and her head whirled – something was badly wrong. She knew before he spoke, knew that something had happened to Sam.

"I'm sorry, Susan..." he paused and bit his lip.

"A fire?" she whispered. "He's been injured in a fire? The thing she most dreaded had actually happened.

"I'm so sorry."

"So where is he?" she swallowed painfully.

"He's at the Radcliffe. He was overcome by smoke, they tried to revive him, but it was no good."

"No! He's not dead? He can't be!"

"I'm afraid so. Can I fetch someone to be with you?"

"Mum..." Somehow she managed to tell him her mother's address.

He nodded. "Bert's outside with the engine. I'll ask him to get her. Then I'll make you a cuppa."

The door close behind him.

Tears running down her face she picked John out of his playpen, hugging him to her. "We're all on our own now, John."

He struggled in her embrace, trying to get down again to play with his toy soldiers.

Pete returned. Soon she was sipping hot sweet tea. Sam had kissed her goodbye only a few hours ago, it seemed impossible that he could be dead. Oh, why should this happen to her? First, jilted, then this.

In a blur she realised her mother was with her – seeing to John and making her more hot sweet tea. She was even taken to the Radcliffe's chapel to say goodbye to the stiff effigy that didn't resemble her Sam. None of this registered with her. Soon it became time for Sam to return from work. She kept waiting to hear his key turn in the lock. Waited in vain. It just couldn't be possible that something like this should ever happen to her; that she was now a widow!

* * *

Later that day, as Roger on his way home from work; passing a newsagents, he saw something on a billboard outside, that halted him in his tracks:

FIREMAN'S TRAGIC DEATH

'Sam Walker , aged 28 was killed in a house fire in Headington yesterday. The fire was started in a chip pan that was accidentally left on by the elderly resident. Having rescued the woman Sam Walker went back into the house to try to rescue the woman's pet dog, but was overcome by smoke, losing his life.'

He read the headline again, hardly able to believe his eyes. Sam Walker, wasn't Susan's husband called Sam Walker? Of course, there could be dozens of Sam Walker's around, but he knew that Susan had married a fireman so in all likelihood this fireman who'd died was her husband. And so it had turned out to be.

* * *

In an effort to support Susan and her parents in their loss, Roger's mum and dad went to the funeral. He didn't know what he could do himself. He couldn't attend the funeral. But should he send Susan a condolence card? In the end he decided to do just that, offering her his deepest sympathy. If anyone should know how she must be feeling, he did. Knew exactly what she would be going through at this moment. As he dropped the card into the postbox he wondered what her reaction would be when she realised it was from him. Would she just rip up the card? He couldn't blame her if she did. He wondered how she would manage on her own with the boy. He supposed she would get a widow's pension, but would she be paid some compensation from the fire service? He guessed her parents would do all they could to help her. But how much could they do? They weren't rich; were only working class like his own parents were.

He never heard anything back as regards his condolence card. Even when Mr & Mrs Swift came to play cards they never mentioned the card he'd sent to Susan. But a few weeks later, as he was walking along the Botley Road to visit the Post Office he saw her coming towards him pushing a pushchair. In it, was a chubby, fair haired boy of about three years of age.

Their eyes met. "Susan?" he ventured. She'd altered slightly having put on a little weight. But then he supposed he might not look exactly the same as he once had. After all, it was years since they were last face to face.

"Roger." She hesitated, her pace slowing. "I'm... I'm so sorry to hear of your loss."

"I'm so sorry to hear of yours." He chucked the boy under his chin. He made up his mind. "Look, can we go for a coffee, to talk over old times, there's a café just along here."

"I don't think so," she said faintly.

"If you're sure?" He swallowed his disappointment.

"I am."

But on Sunday, when he decided to go to the service at the Baptist chapel where he had spent so much of his youth, he saw her again. This time she gave him a shy smile. At the end of the service, encouraged by this, he approached her. Before they could speak to each other, her little boy came running out from the Sunday school class in the back room. Stopping short, he seemed to recognise him and grinned cheekily.

"Hello," said Roger, speaking to the child. "You must be John?"

"Yes."

"I'm an old friend of your Mummy's. My name's Roger."

"He ought to call you, Mr Bowler," chided Susan, frowning.

Roger laughed. "You make me sound like my dad. I'd rather answer to Roger." He turned to John. "Sounds more friendly, doesn't it?"

"Yes," agreed John. "Roger."

"Good boy!" He gave him a sixpence to put in his money box.

This seemed to please Susan. And the following Sunday when he asked her to go for a coffee with him one evening, she agreed. A little later, she even agreed to go to the cinema with him, where they'd sat in the back row and he had placed a tentative arm around her shoulders. After this, they'd met up regularly. Both sets of parents once they realised which way the wind was blowing encouraged the match. A few months later, Roger asked her to marry him. "I've still got feelings for you," he confessed, "they never really died, and lately they have been coming to the fore. I know I let you down in the past which I'm very sorry about now, and also it is a bit soon since your Sam and my Belinda died, but if I've learnt anything, it is that life is short, and we've got to make the best of it while we can."

"That's true."

"So what do you say? Your John could do with a dad. A boy needs a man in his life. "

"I know. And he seems to like you, I suppose."

"I certainly like him." On some of their meetings, John

had been present and Roger and John had become firm friends. With Susan's permission he'd started taking the boy fishing and buying him a little fishing net and helping him catch a tiddler with it.

"I'll have to think about it, I can't make up my mind just like that," said Susan, flustered.

With that he had to be satisfied.

* * *

Susan did think about it. He had hurt her badly in the past, but she had to admit she still felt something for Roger. She had loved Sam, but to be honest, not in the same way. She had married him really for security, now, she had a second chance to have the one she really wanted. But should she trust him, he had always been a flirt, and after a bit when their life together became somewhat humdrum, mightn't he be eyeing up someone else?

With Roger's proposal constantly on her mind, she couldn't sleep at night. As the days passed, her mum and dad noticing the dark shadows beneath her eyes became concerned that she might be ill.

At last, she made up her mind. She would marry Roger, she didn't want to spend the rest of her life on her own. They were strolling along the tow path, and admiring the weeping willows that overhung the river on the opposite bank. She turned to him. ""I've made my decision, Roger."

"And what is it?"

"I've decided to say 'Yes."

"Great!" He took her into his arms and kissed her soundly. "You'll not regret it," he said.

At his words, recalling his past actions, a little thought ran through her head. I hope not!

* * *

Both sets of parents when they learnt about the proposed wedding were thrilled. In fact, they eagerly began making plans for it. And so, on a sunny Saturday in April 1948, Roger and Susan were married at New Road Baptist Chapel, with a party for friends and relatives at Susan's home afterwards. The happy couple then left by train for Winchcombe, a sleepy village near Cheltenham for a couple of days honeymoon (Susan's mother looking after John while they were away) where they stopped at the Post Office in the main street, the Post Mistress letting rooms to holidaymakers.

On their return, Roger moved into Susan's house which was just off the Botley Road. Having received a reasonable sum in compensation from the fire service, she had paid off the mortgage that Sam had taken out.

It wasn't long before Roger learnt he was to become a father. He was thrilled. To think he had thought that he would never actually have a child of his own. He wondered if it would be a boy or a girl, he didn't really care as long as it was healthy.

The months passed. Spring turned to summer. In the warm sunshine, Susan bloomed with impending motherhood. Roger had applied to adopt John. He was a lively happy child and Roger had grown to love him – he couldn't wait to receive the news from the courts that he was actually his dad. At last, what he was longing to hear arrived – John was officially his son. He was delighted, once the new baby was born they would be a proper family. In the meantime, he and Susan took John to the Botley Road Recreation Ground. The same park which he had played in as a boy. Roger pushed John on the swings, and played ball with him on the grass. He also bought him water wings and taking a picnic with them they took John to Tumbling Bay open air swimming baths; also the Hinksey open air baths.

At first, John was a bit nervous of the water, but Roger went in with him and before very long John had forgotten his fear and could do a doggy paddle. Susan would dry him with the towels they'd taken with them and then they would enjoy their picnic.

Summer turned to autumn, and Roger bought his son fireworks which he let off for him, and Susan made him a guy which they placed on top of a bonfire. Their baby was due in January 1949. Both grandmothers were eagerly knitting, the expected child would have enough matinee coats and booties to clothe half a dozen babies. Life finally seemed good.

* * *

Not so good, though for Alec. He still hadn't had any success with getting himself a girlfriend – he was getting fed up at having so many knock backs. One evening though, his luck changed when he was on his way home from seeing a film at the Regal Cinema in Magdalen Road, which was just off the Cowley Road. Suddenly, he heard a sharp cry and saw a girl trip up and fall heavily onto the pavement. He automatically came to her aid, helping her up. "Are you badly hurt?"

"Think I've grazed my knee." She examined it. "And laddered my stocking," she added ruefully.

He picked up the red shoe which had three inch heels. "You'll not be able to walk in this."

She took the shoe from him. "I've only gone and broken the heel. How can I get home with a bad knee and only one shoe? They were my favourite pair of shoes too, though I suppose they're not very practical."

Far from it, though Alec, though he never voiced his thoughts.. "Look," he said, "if you lean on me I can help you along. Where did you live, is it very far away?"

"Not really." She told Alec her address.

With him supporting her, they eventually reached her street and her house.

"Thanks for helping me." She reached up and kissed his cheek.

Flustered, he replied. "That's okay." He noticed she was quite attractive with dark hair. He made up his mind, she could only say 'no'. Somehow, he managed to pluck up enough courage to say, "You wouldn't care to come out with me one evening, would you? Perhaps to the cinema or a drink?" he added hopefully.

"I'd like that."

"You would! Great! When do you suggest?"

"How about tomorrow evening. Would that be suitable to you?"

He felt like dancing a jig. "Certainly would!"

"That's settled then. By the way my names Charlotte, Charlotte Grange. What's yours?"

"Alec, Alec Bowler."

"It's a date then, Alec."

A date, he thought, this looked hopeful. "I'll come and call for you tomorrow evening, what time shall I come?"

"How about 6.30 pm. I get home from work around 6pm, and it gives me time to get changed."

"All right. It's a date then."

She smiled. "Yes. Goodnight, Alec."

"Goodnight, Charlotte."

He was whistling as he left her to get his bus home.

CHAPTER TWENTY

The young woman awoke and opened her eyes. She was lying in bed, but where was she? And more importantly, who was she? She couldn't remember. She definitely couldn't remember anything! Frightened, she began to shiver. Was this loss of memory temporary? Or would she remain in this foggy state forever?

Seeing her stirring, a young woman in a white coat came over. "You're awake. That's brilliant! How do you feel?"

How did she feel? She wasn't certain. She ran her hands up her arms and legs. She didn't seem to have any pain anywhere. "I don't really know," she whispered. "How long have I been here? I really can't remember a thing. And where am I, anyway?"

The nurse looked concerned. "You're at the St Cecilia Nursing Home, hon, and as for how long you've been here, well, some months. You were unconscious when you were found."

"Found! Found where?"

"On top of a haystack which was surrounded by debris, some distance from here. It was just after a tornado hit the area. You must have been lifted up and blown quite a way and the haystack broke your fall – prevented you from having any serious injury. If you had landed on a harder surface, or in water, you most probably wouldn't have survived. So it was fortunate."

"It doesn't feel fortunate to have lost my memory."

"Possibly not. Look, I'm Jean, if you can't even remember your name we'll call you Dorothy for now – like the girl in 'The Wizard of Oz'. I don't suppose you remember that, it's a film. "

Dorothy shook her head.

Jean continued. "Your memory may come back, it often does. I've seen it happen with a couple of other patients who have lost their memory. A sudden shock can trigger it. Now, I'd best got the doctor to examine you, and once he is satisfied with your condition and that it's okay for you to eat, I'll fetch you some solid food. While you've been unconscious you have been fed intravenously." She indicated some tubes and a glass bottle above the bed which she disconnected. She then fetched the doctor- in-charge, an elderly man who examined Dorothy. He seemed quite pleased with her physical state. When he had left Jean brought her a tray containing steak, eggs and French fries. "Enjoy," she said.

To her surprise, Dorothy found that she was really hungry, and she cleared her plate..

At first, of course, with being in bed for so long, she had to be careful when trying to walk. But as the days passed her mobility returned and she was able to help the nurses fetch and carry for some of the other patients. She soon learned there were quite a few of the inmates in this Nursing Home; probably placed there by their families, as some of them had rather erratic behaviour problems which the families obviously couldn't cope with. These male and female patients would often attack the other patients and even members of staff.

There was one young woman called Angel. Whether this was really her name, Dorothy didn't know. She certainly didn't act like an angel, the opposite in fact. She was forever having a tantrum about something. They were having a meal in the dining hall and Angel suddenly got upset and crying and cursing threw her plate, followed by herself on to the floor.

Dorothy went over to help her up and Angel struggled and pushed her away. She fell and banged her head. Something seemed to click in her brain at this and the fog of her memory cleared. "I'm Belinda, Belinda Bowler," she gasped, as she was helped to her feet. "My husband is Roger Bowler, formerly of the Royal Air Force in England. I was living in Mount Olive when a tornado struck. The last thing I remember is a loud roaring and the house shuddering around me."

Within a few hours the rest of her memory returned, that of her parent's farm in Gulf Shores, her time in England, and Oxford, her husband, Roger's home. She also recalled the last few hours before the tornado struck, and Hank. Poor Hank; when the house had blown away what had happened to him? Was he dead? Or had a miracle occurred with him as it had with her? Could he be alive somewhere? She supposed she might never know.

Eventually, she was discharged from St Cecilia's and with some money given her by the doctor in charge, she travelled by Greyhound bus to Gulf Shores and her parents' farm. She alighted and looked around taking in the familiar scene, the sunlit fields, the outhouses near the farmhouse which she knew housed livestock. And there, too, was her dad's old ramshackle truck.

Her mother was the first to see her. She'd gasped, shocked, when she'd opened the door to Belinda's knock, "Belinda!!"

"Yes, it is me, Mom."

"It can't be, you're dead and buried! You were killed in that tornado. You must be a ghost."

She laughed. "No ghost, Mom, I am your Belinda."

"But you're buried, here on the farm."

"Not me! It must be someone else. Someone who looked like me."

She explained to her mother all that had happened to her, how after a haystack had broken her fall she had been unconscious for months in a Nursing Home before coming-to and regaining her memory, and that as soon as she was considered well enough to leave the home she'd made her way to her parents' farm.

Convinced, her mother hugged her. Come on in, and I'll make you a dish of Grits, you must be hungry."

"I suppose I am."

Her mother stood over her as she ate. "It's a miracle, that's what it is, you being alive after all this time."

"I suppose it is." Belinda looked around. "Is Roger here, Mom?"

"Roger, no, he returned to England. He couldn't seem to settle here after you died." She corrected herself. "After, he thought you had died."

"I see. I must go there."

"To England? Must you? So soon?"

"My place is with my husband, Mom."

Her mother nodded. "I guess so. Of course, I'd rather you didn't go so far away, and I know Pop will feel the same as me."

"It can't be helped." She frowned. "There's one problem, I've got no money to pay for the passage. Do you think Uncle Stan would be willing to pull strings for me like he did before to get me there free of charge?"

"I don't know, we'll have to ask him. Now, I'll make up your bed, you must be exhausted after your journey here, you can have a few hours' sleep before the others appear."

Later, refreshed, she saw the rest of the family, who once they had managed to believe their eyes greeted her joyfully. Later, that day her mother phoned her Uncle Stan, explaining the situation. He'd said he'd be only too happy to help, but, instead of her having to go by ship to England which would take a week for her to get there; as flights were beginning to become more commonplace, he would see if he could arrange for her to fly instead.

Lying sleepless in bed that night she wondered what Roger's reaction would be when she turned up on the doorstep. She suppose, like her mother he would think he was seeing a ghost. But would he be pleased to see her? To know she was alive? Surely, he would, would be happy to start a new life with her in England: she didn't intend to return to the States permanently, not after being caught up in a tornado and having her near miss – she was lucky not to have been killed!!

Before she left the farm she found the grave of the unknown young woman who was buried there, her family thinking it was her. She stood looking at it. On the tombstone was engraved her name and date of her birth and supposed death. She wondered who the woman in the

144

grave was, and if there was anyone grieving for her? She didn't suppose there was anyway, that anyone would ever know. Now, knowing that she was alive, her parents were on about replacing the tombstone with another which would read:

YOUNG WOMAN KILLED IN A TORNADO
NAME UNKNOWN. '

* * *

Belinda flew from Birmingham Airport, Alabama, to Heathrow Airport, just outside of London, England. Being served during the flight with a meal by a smartly uniformed Air Hostess she thought how different this trip was to those sea voyages she'd endured in the past and not just because it took less time to get to her destination. Then she'd had seasickness to contend with, not to mention what she had suffered that horrific time when the ship she'd been sailing to England on had been torpedoed and she'd ended up in a lifeboat for days on end.

At last, after going through Customs at Heathrow, and taking a bus to Paddington Station she was on a packed train heading for Oxford, where she took a taxi from the station to Bridge Street, Osney. It was fairly early in the morning and the milk cart drawn by a carthorse was clomping along the street, delivering milk, and people were coming from their houses with jugs to be filled. As she paid the taxi driver she looked around at the once familiar terraced street reflecting on how squashed up were the majority of dwellings in the U.K. compared to those in the U.S. As she did so she recognised the back view of her mother-in-law, Mrs Bowler, with a jug in her hand, entering her house.

She knocked on the door. It was opened as she'd expected by Mrs Bowler. The woman's mouth dropped open as she knew it would, and the milk jug fell from her nerveless fingers on to the doorstep where it shattered, a pool of milk running down onto the pavement.

"I'm not a ghost," said Belinda, "I'm very much alive. Can I come in?"

"Belinda! Is it really you? But you're dead – Roger said so!"

"Roger was wrong! It was a mistake. He identified the wrong woman as me – she's buried at my parents' farm."

"She is?"

"She certainly is."

Mrs Bowler shook her head. "I can't believe my eyes. You can't be Belinda."

"Well, I am. I am Belinda. Your son, Roger's wife."

"Oh!" Her face changed colour. "So, so what happened? How did you manage to survive that terrible... what is it that they are called?"

"A tornado. Just luck, I guess."

"So where have you been all this time?"

Belinda explained. "In a Nursing Home. I was unconscious for several months. When I came to it was some time before my memory returned. When it did, I went first to see my parents. They had thought me dead too, thought me a ghost when I appeared at their door. Anyway, enough of that. Where's Roger? Is he here?" She glanced at her watch. "Or has he already left for work?"

Mrs Bowler's eyes slid from Belinda's and she said awkwardly. "He's probably at work, but nowadays he doesn't live here, he lives in Belvedere Street, just off the Botley Road. But that isn't all."

"What else is there?"

"Something that will shock you as much as you appearing out of the blue here has shocked me. I don't know how I'm going to tell you this. "

"Tell me what?"

"You'd best come in. We don't want all the street knowing our business."

She followed her into the living room. So go on then, tell me."

"He thought you dead and has married again."

146

"What!!" She swallowed painfully. This was a nightmare! So Roger had forgotten her sufficiently to marry someone else – why it wasn't even eighteen months since the tornado. "Who has he married? Do I know her?"

Mrs Bowler said awkwardly. "You do and you don't. He's married Susan."

"What! He can't have, she's already got a husband – a fireman, isn't he?"

"He was, but sadly he was killed in a fire about a year ago. Well, I suppose they were both lonely, and they had been engaged in the past."

Belinda's lips tightened. "How could they marry? He's still married to me. He's a bigamist, that's what he is. I ought to report him to the police."

"He's not a bigamist. He's got your death certificate."

"I don't care if he's got a dozen certificates. I'm very much alive. Tell me the address of where they live. I'm going to go and have it out with them."

"Perhaps I shouldn't tell you. "

"Tell me what?"

"I don't want you to upset her in her condition."

"What condition? Is she ill?"

"No, not ill, she's, she's expecting a baby in a week or two's time."

"No!" Her fingers tightly gripped the handle of her bag wishing it was her rival's throat. So this English bitch was about to give her Roger what she had never managed to do herself. It seemed so unfair, that this Susan should be successful when she herself had failed.

"I'm sorry, Belinda," said her mother-in-law, "it's best you know the score before you go rushing round there to face them."

"I'll face them all right!"

"Perhaps I should come with you. Make sure things don't get out of hand?"

"I could strangle the pair of them!"

"I suppose I can understand how you're feeling. Anyway, you'd best wait until this evening when Roger's home from work. Now, I'll make you a meal and you can have a little rest upstairs."

"That's very kind of you but I don't feel like eating or resting." But as she climbed the stairs to the bedroom she had always shared with Roger when he was home on leave, she thought bitterly, to think she could have gone off with Hank. Perhaps she should have done. She didn't think he would have forgotten her in such a short time as Roger obviously had.

* * *

Susan heard the front door open and seconds later, Roger appeared in the doorway of the living room. "Hello, darling," she said, "I've made your favourite for tea, sausages and bubble & squeak. I'll just fetch it from the kitchen." She did just that while Roger seated himself, opposite little John at the table.

Hardly had Roger picked up his knife and fork than there was a loud banging on the front door.

"Who can that be? "

"No idea," said Roger, chewing with pleasure a piece of sausage.

"I'd best go," said Susan. She hurried along the passage. "I'm just coming. There's no need to knock the door down!"

Reaching the front door, she opened it and gasped. It couldn't be, could it? She hadn't had that much to do with her, but she recognised her all right. It was that Yankee who had stolen her Roger from her. She frowned. But she was dead! Behind her was a very apprehensive-looking Mrs Bowler.

Without waiting for an invitation, the Yankee pushed past Susan and ran into the house, shouting, "Roger! Where are you, Roger?"

A dazed Susan, with Agatha Bowler behind her, hurried along the passage, and into the living room, to see Roger, white-faced with shock, and Belinda, flushed with fury, standing opposite each other, with Roger mumbling, "It can't be! You're dead! I must be hallucinating."

"I bet you wish I was just an hallucination?" spat Belinda.

Roger didn't reply.

Seeing Agatha enter the room, John cried, "Granny Bowler, have you brought me sweeties?"

"Not this time, John."

He looked disappointed.

She turned to Susan. "I'm sorry," she said. "I was as shocked as you are when she turned up on my doorstep this morning, I thought she must be a ghost."

"Not me. I'm no spirit, I'm flesh and blood," Belinda said firmly.

"But, I don't understand," gasped Susan.

"Are you thick or what? I never died. It was all a mistake. Roger identified someone else as me. I'm here to claim my husband."

"He's not a parcel! Claim your husband, indeed. And Roger and I are married, and I'm having his child."

Belinda blenched at this. His child! Her rival's words and the sight of her swollen belly as well as the fact that she herself could never do what Susan could do so easily was obviously extremely painful to her. "You can't be married to Roger when I'm still alive," she spluttered. "Your child will just be a bastard."

"What's a bastard, Mummy?" piped up John.

All the adults looked shocked at the little boy's innocent remark. "A bad person, someone who lies or steals," replied Mrs Bowler hastily.

Susan glared at Belinda. "How dare you!"

"I'll dare as much as I like."

"You stole Roger from me. You must have known he was engaged when you met him but that didn't stop you. A decent girl, once they knew the truth of the matter would have dropped him like a red hot coal. "

"Red hot coal! What does she mean? You English do have some funny expressions." Puzzled, Belinda turned to

149

Mrs Bowler who explained the meaning of the words. She turned to Roger. "So what do you intend to do?"

He ran his fingers through his hair. "Do? What do you mean?"

"You can't stay with her now you know I'm alive. You'd best come back to your mother's. Then we need to see a solicitor to sort all this muddle out."

Susan burst into tears. "You can't leave me, Roger, not when I'm like this. You can't leave me for this Yankee." She ran her hand over her belly.

"He'd better," said Belinda. "And I'll have you know I'm not a Yankee, I'm from the South; I'm a Southerner." She could tell by Roger's face that her appearing out of the blue had put him in a terrible quandary. Was he thinking that perhaps once the authorities knew she was who she said she was, that he ought to divorce her and make his life with Susan? After all, she would be the one with his child.

"All you Americans are Yankees to me," cried Susan. Suddenly, she bent double, "Ow!"

Mrs Bowler frowned. "What's the matter?"

"It's the baby. I think it might be coming."

"But you're not due for nearly another month," stated Roger.

"Well, I think I've started, and she pulled another face and, crying, "Ow!" bent double again. She went outside to the lavatory, and when she returned, she said, "I've had a show, the baby is definitely coming."

"You'd best ring for the midwife," said Mrs Bowler to Roger. She turned to Susan. "Have you got plenty of newspapers to put over the mattress to protect it?"

"I've been saving them. Like you and my mum told me to," she replied, bending double again, "Ow!" She straightened up, relieved. "It's eased a little now, thank goodness. "I'm grateful for the spaces between the pains, it would be awful if they were continuous. But as for the newspapers, the midwife says it's best to cover the mattress with a rubber sheet." She bent double and cried out again. "The pains are coming quite quickly now."

Without bothering with his overcoat, despite it being almost December and pouring with rain outside, Roger dashed out to the telephone box at bottom of the street.

He returned, soaking wet and gasping for breath. "She'll be here as soon as possible."

"Good!" said Mrs Bowler. She turned to Susan. "I've got your bed ready you best come upstairs."

Susan was undressed and in bed by the time the midwife, riding her bicycle, appeared. She wore a long black coat, black stockings and black flat heeled shoes, with a black hat on her head. With her she had an emergency pack which would have been delivered to Susan nearer to her expected time of birth. This, she had been told previously by the midwife would contain dressings and instruments, and also a rubber sheet to cover the mattress on the bed. Removing her coat and hat, and revealing her navy uniform and white apron with a small watch hanging from the left-hand-side of the bib; the midwife immediately instructed Roger to boil as much water as he could and bring it up to the bedroom. This was to wash her hands in and also her instruments, and also to wash the baby and the mother once she was delivered. While he was engaged with doing this, she told Susan to sit on a chair while she recovered the newspapers on the bed with the rubber sheet.

Mrs Bowler made them all tea and they settled down to wait for the birth, with Roger smoking cigarette after cigarette; all of them flinching every time they heard the agonising screams from upstairs.

Eventually, the midwife appeared with a rather worried expression on her face. "There's something wrong with your wife, Mr Bowler. In my opinion, she has a post-partum low-lying placenta."

Belinda, swallowing a mouthful of tea almost choked at hearing the words 'your wife' and knowing the midwife wasn't referring to her.

"I think it's best she goes into the Radcliffe," continued the midwife, "they have got all the right equipment at the

Nuffield Maternity Home. Will you go down to the phone box and ring the hospital and ask for an ambulance?"

He blenched. "Of course." The front door slammed behind him. Within ten minutes of his return, the ambulance, siren blaring was at their door. With Susan, the midwife beside her, it raced through the streets of Oxford, and Susan was very relieved when they arrived at the Radcliffe Infirmary. She was glad she was going into the Nuffield Maternity Home, especially in these circumstances. She had had her first baby, little John there. The Maternity Home had been built in 1931 and was the most up- to- date Maternity Hospital in the country. The money to build it had been donated by Sir William Morris, the owner of the car factory at Cowley, and who later became Lord Nuffield. It had been opened by Queen Elizabeth, the wife of King George V1, when she was the Duchess of York.

Susan was taken into the delivery room, where she was examined by the doctor. He consulted with another of his colleagues, both of them deciding that she had low maternal haemoglobin levels at the start of labour. This could lead to a serious haemorrhage once the child was born.

After several agonising hours, her little girl was born. Though small, with being a month early, the doctor decided that the baby was healthy, but that she should go into an incubator for a while as a precaution.

Before this happened, Susan held her baby in her arms. She was so happy, her little girl was perfect. In her mind's eye she visualized the future. Surely, Roger would stay with her, after all, she was the mother of his child. In these very difficult circumstances hopefully his marriage to the Yankee could be annulled, leaving him free to remarry her. Yes, that was what would happen, she thought happily. She relinquished her baby to the midwife so she could be placed into an incubator. Lying back, she began to daydream. seeing herself pushing the pram containing her little girl to the Botley Road Recreation Ground, with

Roger beside her, and little John running on ahead. She could almost feel the hot sunshine on the back of her neck. The daydream ended abruptly as she realized that something was happening to her between her legs; she was flooding. She looked down, the bottom sheet beneath her was bright red and the room around her was becoming hazy. She weakly called the nursing staff to come to her aid. They came running. The midwife who had delivered her took in the situation immediately. "She's haemorrhaging!"

Pulling Susan's legs apart, she began massaging and pummelling her uterus in an effort to stop the bleeding. To no avail.

"I'll stop, shall I, it's no good, is it?"

"No, what a pity, she was only young. And with such a lovely baby too."

Reluctantly, the two midwives covered Susan's face with the sheet. She was dead.

CHAPTER TWENTY ONE

Roger held his little daughter in his arms and pressed a gentle kiss on to her forehead. He'd got a child of his own at last, but at what a price. She opened her eyes and looked up at him, with the blue eyes that so reminded him of Susan's and gurgled. A couple of months had passed, and his and Susan's baby was home with him and John who seemed pleased to have a little sister. Whenever she dropped her dummy out of her mouth, he would lean over to the pram and replace it for her before she started to cry. Roger had decided to call his daughter, Susan after her mother. It was the least he could do for the poor girl who had tragically lost her life. He put the baby back into her pram. The thoughts that milled around in his head returned. What should he do? His feelings were so mixed up. He knew he had loved Susan, but he also knew that he loved Belinda to whom he was still married – they had sorted things out as she'd wanted and it was now official that she wasn't dead. With this being clarified she had suggested she move into the house with him that he'd shared with Susan. It was true he needed help with the children – he couldn't work and look after John and Susan. It wasn't fair to the two elderly women, his mother and Susan's for them to see permanently to the children. At the moment, they took turns to mind them. He dropped them off (his mother's one week and Mrs Swift's the following week) at the two women's' houses before work each day and picked them up again when he'd finished.

There was a knock at the door. He knew who it would be. Belinda came every evening at around 6pm to put the children to bed. For the time being she was living at his parents' house until they'd decided what they should do about their future. As the bit of money she had brought with her from America was gone, and needing some to pay his mother for her keep, she had gone to the Employment Exchange and found a part time job as a waitress in a nearby cafe.

He opened the door to her. She entered, and immediately went over to John and tickled him under his chin. Roger knew she had always loved children (had been so disappointed that she couldn't become a mother herself) and John and Susan were no exception. He knew she would be a loving mother to them.

"Hi, hon," she said, turning to him. "Have you sold a lot of houses today?"

"One or two," he replied.

After playing for a few minutes with John and his dinky toys; John was running the miniature cars back and forth across the hearth rug and she'd joined in with the game; she lifted Susan from her pram and held her out to Roger. "Say goodnight to Daddy, sweetheart."

Susan gurgled.

"Goodnight darling," said Roger, kissing her tenderly.

Belinda, then took the baby upstairs to bath and get ready for bed.

Next, it was John's turn. He didn't want to leave his cars. "Can't I play a little longer?" he pleaded.

She shook her head and encouraged him to go upstairs by promising she would read him a story once he was in bed.

Half listening to the murmur of Belinda's voice from John's bedroom, Roger's thoughts drifted back to the day of Susan's funeral. He hardly knew now how he got through it. She was buried at Botley Cemetery, in the same grave as her late husband, Sam, who had lost his life less than eighteen months earlier. He had placed a red rose on the grave before leaving the cemetery for the funeral tea at Mr. & Mrs. Swift's home.

His thoughts turned to his younger brother, Alec. Alec, he knew had been very upset to learn that Susan had died – he'd always had a soft spot for her. At Susan's funeral at Botley Cemetery, Alec had had a job to hold back his tears, though no more than Roger, or any of the other mourners – especially his mother – she'd always wanted

Susan as a daughter. She must have thought all her dreams had come true when he and Susan were married. Then to have it all dashed away. Susan had been so young – only twenty five, she should have had the rest of her life before her. His thoughts returned to Alec again. All the same, as far as his youngest brother was concerned, life had lately taken a turn for the better. He was at last courting seriously, and Roger guessed, to his mother's relief, Alec's girlfriend seemed a respectable girl who lived in a good neighbourhood of Oxford, Henley Street, just off the Iffley Road. Alec had taken Charlotte home for tea last Sunday, and according to Wilfred's wife, Janet who had also been there with Wilfred and their children (they had called into see him before returning to Sunningwell) that this Charlotte had offered to help with the washing up afterwards. Something like this he knew, would be in the girl's favour in his mum's opinion.

Roger heard Belinda's footsteps on the stairs. Having seen to the children, she would be, as she usually did, coming downstairs to listen to the wireless with him for a few hours, before going back to his mother's house. She entered the room. "Shall I make us a pot of tea first before we listen to the wireless, hon?" She'd recently started drinking tea, too. Laughingly, she'd said, If I'm going to be English, I may as well do what the English do!"

Roger smiled. "That would be lovely."

She went out to the kitchen. He heard the rattling of crockery. Shortly after this, she returned carrying a tray, on it, a pot of tea, milk jug, sugar basin, and two cups and saucers. The tea was poured, the wireless turned on to their favourite station.

He turned it off again.

"Why did you do that?"

"Because I need to talk to you."

"What about?" she queried.

"I think we should approach Reverend Unsworth at the Chapel. "

"Why?"

"After me being married to Susan; or at least I thought I was married to her, you and I both feel awkward about us living together again, despite the fact that as you never really died, we are still technically husband and wife."

"That's true. But what can we do about it?"

"I've heard you can renew your wedding vows. And that's what I want to talk to the Reverend Unsworth about."

"That's a good idea," said Belinda. "Let's do it. The sooner the better."

"Right, that's settled." He turned to her, and taking her into his arms, tentatively kissed her – the first time they had kissed since before that devastating tornado. Feeling encouraged by her response the kiss deepened.

Eventually, withdrawing reluctantly from each other, he said, "We'll have a word with him after the Service on Sunday morning."

* * *

The ceremony for the renewal of Roger's and Belinda's wedding vows was all arranged for Sunday morning the 5th of May, 1949. Afterwards, there was to be a party at the Democrat Club. All of Roger's old friends from the R.A.F. who had survived the war were invited, amongst them, Lionel and Charlie. As Roger wrote out the invitations he thought of Ben. How he wished he could be present, but when he'd enquired about him he'd been told that he had been killed in 1943. Also to be invited was Olivia, whom Belinda had worked with at the Serviceman's Club and who had remained in England at the end of the war, and her good friend, Gillian and her husband, Jimmy, whom these days, still lived in Lincolnshire

That Sunday morning, as she got herself ready in a fetching cream-and-yellow New Look dress by Dior, with its neat waist-hugging jacket and long full skirt, she suddenly thought of Hank. Was he alive somewhere? She hoped so. She also hoped he was as happy as she was, that he had found love with someone else who was free to love him as he deserved. She had never told Roger that Hank was with her when the wooden house had blown away. It was best she didn't. She didn't want to start off his jealousy again.

Roger had bought himself a car, and he came and picked her up from his parents' house and drove her to the New Road Baptist Chapel. After the Service and the final hymn, the Reverend Unsworth announced. "Roger and Belinda, whom you all know are going to renew their marriage vows." He turned to them. "Do you, Roger take this woman to be your lawful wedded wife....?"

"I do," he replied, giving her a look of love.

Then it was her turn. She felt as nervous as she had on that long ago at her parents' farm.

"Do you, Belinda, take Roger to be your lawful wedded husband…"

"I do," she replied. She knew she was doing the right thing. She loved Roger more than she'd ever thought possible, and they would be a proper family with two small children to love and care for.

"You may kiss the bride," said the Reverend Unsworth.

Roger did just that to loud applause and cheers from the congregation.

CHAPTER TWENTY TWO

Roger was listening to the early morning news on the wireless. It was the 5th of February 1952. Suddenly the newscaster, John Snagge said, "This is a special announcement."

Roger turned to where seven- year-old, John and four-year-old, Susan were seated at the table and supposed to be eating their breakfast cereal, but in fact, were again squabbling with each other. "Shush kids!" He turned up the volume and listened carefully. Special announcement! This could be important!

"Last night," said John Snagge, "King George V1 died at Sandringham House. He'd retired in his usual health, but passed away in his sleep and was found dead in bed at 7.30am, by a servant."

"Dead!" Roger gasped, shocked. He couldn't have been that old. He recalled the time at the Palace when he had received his medal from the King. Though he'd a slight stutter, his Majesty certainly had a certain presence about him – Kingly, that was what it was. He went over to the sideboard and opened one of the drawers. He removed a small velvet-covered box. He opened it, and took out the silver medal which he was so proud of. He fingered reverently the still shiny surface. This medal was to go to John when he died – he being the eldest son.

He heard Belinda enter the room, as usual at this hour of the morning, she was wearing a long housecoat over her nightdress. With her having been present when he'd received the medal, she too, would remember the king and be sad about his passing.

"What's wrong? And why have you found out your medal?"

He lifted his head and turned to her. "I've just heard it on the wireless. "The King's died."

"What! When?"

He told her of John Snagge's announcement.

She shook her head in disbelief. "Never!"

"Unfortunately, it's true."

"That's awful. Poor Queen Elizabeth, and the princesses. They'll be devastated at losing their husband and father. I suppose Princess Elizabeth will now be queen. What a responsibility for such a young woman. Though I guess she'll be given some support from Prince Philip. Not to mention the government. "

"She'll need it! They're on holiday in Kenya at the Treetops Hotel. They'll be coming back here straight away, I imagine."

"Possibly they've left already."

"Could have, though it won't take them long by air."

"What a way to end a holiday," reflected Belinda.

"Yes, in the midst of life…." He patted his tummy. "Anyway, how about some breakfast?"

"Bacon and eggs coming up, hon," she replied. She turned to the children. "If you've finished your breakfast, John, go and get ready for school."

For once, he obediently got down from the table and ran out of the room and up the stairs. She then headed back to the kitchen.

* * *

Over the next few days Roger constantly listened to the wireless and read the newspapers. He heard on the wireless that Princess Elizabeth had returned from Kenya on the 7th of February, and that she had been proclaimed Queen the following day, the 8th of February. He also read in the Oxford Mail that the King's body was to lie in state for three days in Westminster Hall. A few days later he read that during this period about 300.000 people had filed past the coffin to pay their respects. Reading this, he was glad that he had taken some time off work to go to London to be one of them.

After a State Funeral, King George V1 body was interred in Westminster Abbey.

Soon everywhere was talking about the crowning of young Queen Elizabeth 11. The Coronation was to be held the following year, on the 2nd of June 1953. It was to be a national holiday.

"We'll need to get a television set so we can watch the Coronation," he said to Belinda.

"Good idea! What about your mum and dad. Shall we invite them to come and see it with us?"

"We could do. Or we could buy them a set as well, they'll then have entertainment to fill the long winter evenings. "

Belinda thought this a good idea so he did just this, getting two televisions sets from Taphouses in the High Street. As it was a case of two sets, he got them at a discount. He then took one of the sets to his parents' house in Bridge Street and set it up in their front room. He had to smile at his mother's face when she saw the set.

"You just turn the knob on the front to turn it on," he explained.

"What if it explodes?"

"It won't! Go on, try turning it on."

But she wouldn't attempt it and his dad had to be the one to turn it on. She stared transfixed at the image on the screen of Muffin the Mule. Both he and his dad had to laugh at her expression.

"She'll get used to it," said Roger.

And so she did, and by the following June, and the Coronation itself, she was turning it on and off with no bother at all.

* * *

Agatha felt almost like a queen herself with being the owner of a television set. She knew a few people in the street had bought one so they could watch the Coronation, but not everyone. She knew for a fact that Mrs Paxton, next door hadn't got one. She would have made sure Agatha knew about it if she had obtained a set. So seeing her at her front door one morning, Agatha said proudly, "Would you and Fred like to come in and see the Coronation on our television? We've got one, you know."

Mrs Paxton's face lit as if an electric light had been switched on. "We certainly would! That's very good of you. I'll bring some sausage rolls and pork pies to eat while we watch it."

And I'll supply some of my little fruit cakes, and cups of tea, of course."

"Wonderful! Who would have thought that we'd all be able to see such a great occasion as this without even having to travel all the way to London. It's a modern miracle, this invention!"

"It certainly is!"

And so it was arranged.

The morning of Tuesday 2nd of June dawned, bright and sunny to match the great occasion. At about ten o'clock the Paxtons' arrived, as well several other neighbours that Agatha had invited who also hadn't got a television set.

Everyone seated themselves eagerly around the television, and Agatha, without any help from George, proudly turned it on. A picture of the London streets appeared which were lined with well-wishers and loyal subjects, all enthusiastically waving Union Jacks, as a golden coach, carrying the queen and drawn by white horses came into view

The coach stopped outside the Abbey Church of St Peter, Westminster. Her Majesty alighted, she was wearing a white satin dress which the newscaster informed them had been designed and made by Norman Hartnell, the white satin having been obtained from Lady Hart Dyke's silk farm at Lullington Castle. The skirt was backed with cream taffeta throughout and reinforced with three layers of horsehair. This additional support gave the skirt a certain stability which dispersed the weight of the beading over the whole of the bell shape, making it as light as air to wear. As a small omen for good fortune, Norman Hartnell had also embroidered an extra four-leaved Shamrock on the left side of the dress.

At the sight of this wonderful dress, everyone in the room, gasped in delight, "Doesn't she look lovely!" exclaimed Mrs Paxton.

Even the men enthusiastically agreed.

A further coach, which had carried the Maids of Honour and followed that of the queen's drew to a halt. They too alighted; then got into position to carry the six-yard long Robe of State of crimson, velvet edged with ermine and with two rows of embroidered gold lace and gold filigree work, which was attached to the queen's shoulders

Slowly, to the strains of organ music, the queen and the Maids of Honour made their way into the abbey and along the nave, which was surrounded on either side by hundreds of invited guests, to where the Archbishop of Canterbury was waiting.

The service began, with its usual prayers and hymns. At last came the moment when the queen was actually crowned by the Archbishop. The crown was the seven-pound St Edward's crown that had been made in 1661.

A great cheer went up from the congregation as he placed it carefully onto her head.

"Looks heavy!" summed up Mrs Paxton. "I wonder she can keep her head upright with such a weight on it!"

"I wouldn't fancy wearing such a weight," put in Mrs Biggs, who lived three houses away from Agatha, "not even to be queen!"

As Queen Elizabeth 11, and the rest of the royal party, accompanied by their guests left the abbey to the sound of the abbey's musical bells, Agatha brought in the refreshments from her kitchen, and they all toasted with tea their new queen, before tucking into their own celebratory feast.

CHAPTER TWENTY THREE

Wilfred was seated next to the wireless checking his football coupon. Suddenly, he grinned, leapt out of his chair and shouted, "Janet! Janet!"

She came running from the kitchen where she was washing up. "Good God!" she exclaimed, "what on earth is it? Are you feeling poorly?"

The grin on his face widened even more. "We'll never be poor again, I reckon."

"Never be poor. What do you mean?" she asked puzzled.

He examined his coupon again. "I think I've won quite a bit of money."

"How much?"

"I don't know we'll have to wait to find out."

"How long will we have to wait?"

"When the Pools people notify us."

Hearing the raised voices their two children, which unusually for them were sitting quietly in the next room playing a game of snakes and ladders, came running in too. What's going on?" asked Maureen.

"Yes, what's going on?" repeated Ralph.

"Your dad has only gone and won a considerable sum on the Pools," said Janet.

"Great! Can I have a party dress? I've been invited to my friend, Jill's birthday party."

"Great! Can I have a model train set?"

"And I'd like a twin-tub washing machine. Mrs Brigg's next door has got one and she reckons it makes doing the washing much easier"

"Calm down," laughed Wilfred. "Let's wait until we know what kind of money we are talking about. I might have got it wrong – it might only be ten shillings."

All three faces fell. "Ten shillings, but you said it was a lot of money," grumbled the girl.

"You'll have to wait and see. I can't buy party dresses,

train sets, or twin tubs until I know."

With that they all had to be satisfied.

They heard the following day, when Wilfred received a letter from the Pools people. It was a great deal of money, more than Wilfred had certainly ever imagined owning - £10,000.

At this, delighted, all the family danced a jig around the living room. A few days later, as arranged, the Pools people accompanied by the Press came and took a photograph of Wilfred outside their house holding the cheque. This photograph was to appear in the Oxford Times.

After the Pools people and the photographer had left, he turned to his family. "The first thing I'm going to do is buy this house. I've always fancied owning my own house and we won't have to pay rent anymore, which will be quite a saving."

"That's true, but what if the landlord doesn't want to sell it to us," said Janet.

"We'll have to ask him, we won't know unless we do. Will we?"

Wilfred contacted their landlord. He was happy to sell the house to him, to the tune of £2,000. Wilfred, then put the deeds into his bank, along with the remaining £8,000 for safe keeping. That evening, he turned to Janet. "You know, I've always wanted to start my own plumbing business instead of working for someone else, so now I can."

"Well, as long as I get my housekeeping from you every week, I'm pleased for you to be able to realise your ambition."

After this, there was a spending spree. He bought his family all that they wanted, as well as new clothes for everyone.

"So what are you going to do with the rest of it," asked Janet. "Is there anything else you are thinking of getting?"

"I will, of course, put some of it by for a rainy day, but I thought I'd help out our Alec and that poor little lad they've got."

"What a good idea! I don't know how Charlotte copes with him? It must be very hard. So what were you thinking of doing for him?"

Alec and Charlotte, after a courtship of two years had been married in 1951. Charlotte had been left a few hundred pounds by her grandmother, so with this, they had a small deposit and were able buy a terraced house in St Clements.

"Paying for them to have an extension built on to their house, especially adapted to his needs," said Wilfred.

A year after their marriage, Charlotte had become pregnant. Both she and Alec were thrilled. The child, a little boy, was born on January 9th 1953, the same year that the queen was crowned, which they named George after Alec's father. But at three weeks little George was rushed into the Radcliffe Infirmary with pneumonia. He was immediately put into an oxygen tent and was fed intravenous with a tube up his nose. It looked like touch and go for a while. Charlotte had been breast-feeding him and when he had improved a little, she would express her milk at home, and take it to the Radcliffe where they would sterilize it and put it in a bottle so that the nurse could feed him with it.

At three months, he was well enough to come home. Both Alec and Charlotte thought all their troubles were over. But all was not right with George, he was having chest infections after chest infections. At ten months, he had to be taken to the Radcliffe for a chest x-ray. While there, Charlotte said to the doctor, "Shouldn't he be pulling himself up by now in the pram?"

"Perhaps, he's going to be retarded," replied the doctor, offhandedly.

Charlotte was shocked by his blasé remark. But as the months passed it was obvious that something was radically wrong with George – he still couldn't sit up on his own. Eventually, she and Alec were told that he was brain-damaged and would probably never walk. And although

Charlotte rubbed him all over every day with olive oil, hoping it might do his muscles some good, and had even got him a baby bouncer, there was never any improvement in his condition.

The following evening, Wilfred knocked at Alec's door. He opened it. Seeing who it was he said, "Well, I was beginning to think that you had forgotten our address."

Wilfred looked shamefaced. "You know how it is. Not enough hours in the day to do all that needs to be done what with work and the family. Anyway, I've had a bit of luck and that's why I'm here."

"Well, that's wonderful, come on in and tell me and Charlotte all about it. She's upstairs at the moment seeing to George."

"He will be a bit heavy to carry up there before long."

"Yes, but what else can we do?"

Wilfred seated himself in an armchair. That's why I'm here."

"What do you mean?"

"As I said, I've had a bit of luck, won a decent sum of money on the Pools."

"Have you, you've always been a jammy one, I've done the Pools for years and only ever won a few shillings."

"It's a decent sum," said Wilfred, "and I've decided, if you and Charlotte will agree to it, to pay out for an extension for George especially adapted to his needs."

Alec's face lit up. "That's great of you, and Janet, of course."

They heard Charlotte's step on the stairs.

"Charlotte, come here! I've got something wonderful to tell you."

She appeared. "What is it? She registered Wilfred. She said, wryly, "Long time no see."

"I'm sorry about that," said Wilfred.

Then she took in Alec's beaming face. What's going on?"

"He's only going to pay for us to have an extension for our George."

"Is he, well, that's wonderful, but I don't understand. Where's the money coming from?"

"I've had a big win on the Pools."

* * *

So Alec applied to the Town Hall for planning permission for an extension to be built at the back of their house, with a bedroom containing an electric hoist over the bed, and a specially adapted bathroom. All the Councillors turned up to view the proposed site. A week or so later, planning permission was granted. Alec, had left the Electric Light works some years before and was now a painter and decorator. He planned to do the interior work himself, such as making the window frames and doors and fitting them. Wilfred, being a plumber agreed to do any plumbing that was needed, free of charge, and Roger, not to be outdone, agreed to do the labouring.

A couple of months later, the shell of the extension was up, and within another couple of month, the interior was also completed and Alec and Charlotte were able to move George into his new accommodation.

CHAPTER TWENTY FOUR

It was now 1956 and John was now ten, and Susan, being seven had left the Infants' school and just started at Primary. John thought of Roger as his father, and Susan, thought of Belinda as her mother. Both children knew of their real antecedents. Mostly, John never seemed to worry about this, he was too busy playing with his mates over the Botley Road Recreation Ground – or swimming at Tumbling Bay's open air baths. He had turned out to be rather clever and Roger had great hopes of him winning the scholarship and attending the same school as he had, Oxford Grammar School.

John accepted Susan most of the time – even though she was only a half-sister, and a girl! Both Roger and Belinda knew that at times he was a little jealous of her. She was really Roger's own daughter, his little Princess, whereas his father was actually Sam, the fireman, who had died when he was small. When he'd come home from playing with his mates, his lips would twist in annoyance at the sight of her sitting on Roger's lap and being cuddled by him. All he got from the man he called Dad was his hair ruffled and a, "You okay, my boy?" He got plenty of affection from Belinda, but that just wasn't the same.

Then when Belinda had asked him to take Susan with him and his mates to the Botley Road Recreation Ground he hadn't been at all keen. She was a girl. A sissy, in his book. He had no choice but to take her. Once outside the house he had warned her, "You had better behave yourself when you're with us, unless you want me to pull your pigtails! Do you hear me?"

Susan had flinched at this. Why was he always so mean to her? She noticed a girl about the same age of herself trailing after Sid, one of Roger's mates. She looked as upset as she did herself. Possibly Sid found his little sister as much as an embarrassment as Roger did her. She went up to her, "Hello, I'm Susan, what's your name?"

"Fay," said the girl in reply.

"Would you like to play with me? We could go over to the swings, I could push you, and then you could push me. What do you say?"

Fay smiled. "I'd like that very much."

Reaching the swings, they each took turns on them. Fay going first.

Susan pushed as hard as she could. "Wee," cried Fay as she flew through the air.

Then Fay did the pushing. "Wee," cried Susan, flying through the air.

So after this the two girls, Susan and Fay, palled up and often played together.

* * *

When John was eleven he won the scholarship as Roger had hoped he would. As Roger had also hoped for, he was transferred to Oxford Grammar School. His ambition was the join the R.A.F. like Roger had when he was old enough and hopefully become a pilot. His bedroom walls were plastered with pictures of aircraft, and Roger bought him an Airfix model kit of a Lancaster Bomber. This, they worked on together and which when completed had pride of place on his chest-of-drawers.

Meanwhile, Susan had become a Brownie. Soon, her uniform was covered in badges. When she wasn't at Brownies, or playing with Fay, who was also a Brownie, she would go to Granny and Granddad Bowler's house. One day she saw Granny Bowler sewing some material on her sewing machine. What are you making, Granny?"

"I'm making myself a new summer dress."

"How clever you are. I wish I could make myself a dress."

"Do you really?

"Could you help me to make one?"

"If you're really serious. We'll have to go to the cattle market so you can choose some dress material and a paper pattern."

As it was the school holidays, they were able to go to get the material and the pattern the following Wednesday, Wednesday being the day that the cattle market was always held on. After studying the bolts of material on display Susan chose some pink cotton material which was decorated with small white spots. Later, Granny Bowler helped her pin the pattern to the material and then cut out the sections of the dress which she then tacked together. After a few practises at sewing with the sewing machine and odd bits of material, with Granny Bowler's help, Susan made her first dress.

In Granny and Granddad's bedroom, proudly she pirouetted in front of Granny's cheval mirror, and the skirt swirled out around her. Everyone admired her first attempt at dressmaking. At this, she told everyone that her ambition was to design clothes when she grew up.

At thirteen, she won a scholarship to the Technical College to study art. Life seemed good. Roger had done well at Rumble and Badstocks, and recently been made a partner in the business, and they were able to move into a big house at Boars Hill – a house to rival those houses his mother had worked in as a girl. When she saw the house for the first time they had to gently redirect her before she could head off to the back door to knock for admittance.

Just after this, though, tragedy struck.

There was a knock at the door.

Agatha Bowler was just laying the table for tea – a high tea of kippers and bread and butter, followed by some of her famous small fruit cakes – George's favourite meal. She was expecting him home at any minute. She laid down onto the tablecloth a knife and fork. Who could that be?

She opened the front door, to her surprise, she saw a policeman outside. "Mrs Bowler?" he queried.

"Yes," replied Agatha apprehensively. The policeman looked very serious. Surely he wasn't about to tell her that there was something wrong with one of her boys?

"Can I come inside?"

"Yes, but, why?"

"It's bad news, I'm afraid. Are you on your own in the house?"

"Yes, but…"

"Perhaps a neighbour could come in with you?"

Agatha bit her lip. "She indicated the front door adjacent to her own. "Mrs Paxton, if she's in."

He knocked. Second later, Mrs Paxton opened her door. She too looked startled to see a policeman. "What is it?"

"It's Mrs Bowler," explained the policeman. I've got some bad news to impart to her. Can you spare a few minutes to come into her house while I tell her. She shouldn't be alone."

"Of course." Mrs Paxton pulled her door to and they all went into Agatha's together. The policeman first removing his helmet and placing it beneath his arm. He indicated a chair to Agatha. She, bemused, seated herself.

He cleared his throat. "I'm afraid there's been an accident, Mrs Bowler. Your husband, George Bowler was knocked down by a car as he was leaving the Railway Workshops."

Agatha's face whitened and she wrung her hands together and started to shake. "No! Is he badly hurt? Have they taken him to the Radcliffe? I need to get there – see him."

Mrs Paxton looked shocked. She came over to Agatha and placed an arm around her. "I'm   sorry,"   said   the policeman, "but he's not in the wards. He's… well, he is the Mortuary, you see, I'm afraid he died instantly."

"Dead! No! He can't be – I've just got his Sunday suit dry cleaned for him." She began to sob.

"I'm so sorry, my dear," said Mrs Paxton "I'll make some tea," she offered, at a loss to know what else to do.

"Good idea," agreed the policeman.

Mrs Paxton busied herself with the kettle on the hob and found out teacups. Then, she fetched milk from the meat safe in the kitchen. "Will you have one?" she asked the policeman.

"No, I can't stay. I'll leave her in your capable hands. You'd best notify her family – are any of them on the phone?"

"Her son, Roger will be. I'll get my old man to come in and stay with her while I pop down the street to the shop and get him to phone for me. Roger Bowler works in an Estate Agents, Rumble and Badstocks, they're sure to be in the phone book."

"Good idea." He left.

She made the tea and tried to get Agatha to drink some, but she was too upset to bother. She then went outside and into her own house. Her husband was half asleep, supposedly listening to the wireless. He jerked awake and took in her expression. "What's happened?"

She explained. He agreed to come in next door and stay with Agatha while she went to phone Agatha's son. At the shop she got Mr Bird to phone Rumble & Badstocks. She spoke to Roger who was very shocked and agreed to let his brothers' know. After this, he'd come and take over from her as regards his mother. It was a couple of hours later before Mrs Paxton was relieved and able to return next door.

The funeral was arranged by the brothers, their mother being in no fit state to arrange anything. It was to be held at the New Road Baptist Chapel, and afterwards the internment of the coffin would be at Botley Cemetery.

The night before the body was brought to the house as customary, where it lay on a table in the front room with lit candles at the head and the foot of the coffin. Agatha sat by it all night, kissing the waxen cheek from time to time and sobbing – a pile of sodden handkerchiefs on her lap. Belinda tried to get her to go to bed, saying, she must be worn out, but she wouldn't listen.

The next morning, the undertakers arrived to take the coffin which was covered with dozens of brightly coloured floral wreaths and sprays to the New Road Baptist Chapel. All the female mourners wore deepest black with black hats to match, amongst them was Mr and Mrs Paxton as

Fred Paxton was an old friend of George's having worked with him on the railway. The whole street turned out to see George Bowler, make his final journey – he'd always been very popular as regards his neighbours having often given those of them that weren't so flushed, fruit and vegetables from his allotment.

Roger helped his mother into the car. She was inconsolable again, with a handkerchief pressed to her nose. The car drove past the ancient Castle Mound, all that was left of the ruins of a Norman castle. Registering the Mound that Agatha had seen a million times over the years when walking to the Covered Market in the High Street, she wished with all her heart that she could go back in time to one of those days when she knew that in a short while, her George would be coming home from work.

Eventually, they reached their destination, and followed, two by two, into the chapel. First, went Roger supporting his mother, next came Belinda with Wilfred, after this was Janet with Alec, and Charlotte with John – and all the other mourners, following behind

They seated themselves in the familiar pews. The funeral service was to be taken by the Reverend Unsworth, despite him being in his seventies, he was still the minister of the New Road Baptist Chapel. The service began with the congregation saying the Lord's Prayer together. This was followed by a eulogy given by Roger, he saying, amongst other things, what a good father and friend to everyone George Bowler had always been, and how as a lad, his dad had taken him fishing, which had brought about his life-long love of the sport.

The Reverend Unsworth then announced a hymn. "We will now sing 'The Lord is my shepherd'. To organ music everyone sang the well-loved words, all except Agatha, who broke down after a few words and again began to sob.

"The Lord's my shepherd, I'll not want,
He makes me down to lie,
In pastures green, he leadeth me,

The quiet waters by.
Goodness and mercy all my life
Shall surely follow me,
And in God's house for ever-more,
My dwelling place shall be."

The service ended, and two by two, they filed out of the chapel, where the coffin was again placed in the hearse for the journey to the Botley Cemetery. All the mourners piled into the black limousines and were driven to the cemetery. Once there it was again making their way arm-in-arm to the graveside. Earth was piled up on one side. The coffin was carefully, lowered into the grave to the minister's 'Dust to dust, ashes to ashes....'

All of a sudden, Agatha Bowler dashed forward. "I can't live without George. He was my life. I want to die so I can be with him."

It was obvious to everyone that she meant to throw herself into the grave. Roger and Wilfred grabbed an arm each, preventing her in time.

They returned to their parents' house where a funeral meal had been prepared by Belinda and Janet, with the addition of a few bottles of beer, plus glasses of sherry for the ladies. All the conversation, when it wasn't being drowned out by Agatha's sobbing, was about George, and reminisces about the past flew back and forth. In the kitchen, Belinda and Janet did the clearing away and washing up.

"Do you think it's safe to leave Mother-in-law here on her own?" said Janet.

Belinda shook her head. "No, but what can we do? If she won't come with any of us. Roger's asked her, to come for a little while until she feels more settled in herself, but she's refused. We can't kidnap her."

"Ask her again. Keep on at her until she agrees. It's worth a try, isn't it? I don't think she should be left here on her own."

"I agree. She does seem to be acting rather oddly."

175

This Roger did. But she said she wanted to stay in her own house with her own things.

* * *

Everyone had gone home. The house seemed so quiet, too quiet. Agatha sat in her usual armchair in the living room. Opposite was George's chair – empty!

Confused thoughts ran through her head. Where was he? Was he upstairs? He had to be upstairs. Yes, that was it! She rose and went into the passage, "George," she called urgently as she climbed the stairs. "Are you there?" There was no answer.

Reaching their bedroom, she looked around willing herself to see him, but there was no George!

Feeling desperate now, she went back downstairs and looked all around the ground floor, but she couldn't find him anywhere. She went out into the backyard and searched the coal place and the outside lavatory. No, George. .She then went back inside and upstairs again, still searching. There was no George to be found anywhere. She went up and down the stairs a half a dozen times, but then feeling exhausted, flopped into her armchair and began to cry. She knew now for certain that George was gone. Gone for good!

The following Friday evening she found the playing cards out as she always did and put them ready on the table for when the Swifts came for their usual card game. It was only then, that she realised that though they'd said they would call round to see how she was, without George to make up the foursome, they would never be playing cards ever again. At this, suddenly knowing her present confusion could only become worse, she agreed to take up Roger and Belinda's offer to live with them.

They took her to their house where it was decided she should stay permanently. But all her recent stress led to a stroke, which left her completely helpless. She lingered for a while then had another stroke. She died at the Radcliffe

Infirmary within six months of her husband's demise. This meant another family funeral for the Bowlers'. After a service at the New Road Baptist Chapel. Agatha was laid to rest beside her husband in the Botley cemetery

* * *

Susan and John's other grandparents were becoming frail. Belinda did what she could for them – running a hoover around in their house once a week, and getting shopping in for them. And Roger would take them out for rides in his car. This went on for a year or so, but then Granny Swift also had a stroke and couldn't look after herself or her husband.

One day, when Roger got in from work, having popped in first to see the elderly couple, he said to Belinda. "What do you think, shall we have the Swifts to live with us? After all, they are John's grandparents."

"I don't mind, if you don't mind," she replied.

So they called at their house and suggested this to them.

"I don't know, we don't really want to give up our home, we've lived here for forty years," said Mr Swift.

"I can understand that, but you really can't manage your wife and see to everything else on your own, can you?"

He looked across at her, slumped in her armchair, her eyes vacant. "I suppose not."

Sadly, he eventually agreed that moving to Roger's and Belinda's would be for the best. With this settled, everything was packed up that Granddad and Granny Swift might need and transported to the house at Boars Hill, including some familiar furniture for their bedroom so they would feel at home.

* * *

Both the Swifts were gone by the time John left school at eighteen. He had got over his earlier jealousy of Susan and they'd become almost friends. He'd applied to join the R.A.F. and to his delight, was accepted. He rose swiftly, and eventually, he did become a pilot. Roger was pleased by John realising the ambition that he himself had had in his youth.

When Susan left the Technical she was taken on by a high-class dressmaker in Queen Street. She also rose in her chosen career, and soon her designs were being worn by titled ladies as well as television celebrities.

A year later, John came home with a friend, Victor Black who was also a pilot. When he was introduced to Susan, Victor said to John afterwards. "You never told me you had such a pretty sister?"

"Is she? I'd not noticed."

"You must be blind then!"

Roger and Belinda smiled to themselves knowingly. They could tell by the way Susan and this young man were looking at each other that there would be 'Wedding Bells' before very long.

And so there were. On April the 17th 1972, with Susan, carrying a bouquet of flowers picked from the garden at Boars Hill, and looking so beautiful as she made her vows to Victor, she having designed and made her own wedding dress in cream brocade. She had one bridesmaid, Fay, with whom she was still close friends. She had designed and made the other girl's dress too, which was in lilac taffeta.

The ceremony was conducted by the Reverend Parsons, Reverend Unsworth, having now retired. After the ceremony, everyone went by car to the five star Randolph Hotel in Cornmarket, where a delicious sit-down wedding breakfast was served. Speeches were made by Roger and John, who was Victor's best man. And everyone cheered when the bride and groom together cut the beautiful three-tier iced wedding cake.

Later that evening, Susan and Victor were waved away from Oxford Station on the first leg of their journey to Alabama where they were to stay with Belinda's brothers and sisters and their families. Susan had never been on a plane before and was terribly excited, if a little nervous. Victor had arranged for champagne to be served to them with their meal during the long haul flight. Their flight was uneventful much to Susan's relief, and eventually they touched down in New York, where after a wait of several hours in the airport, they caught their connecting flight to Alabama. Once there, they were welcomed with open arms by Belinda's family who vied with each other to accommodate Susan and Victor in their homes and lavishly entertain them. The newly-wed couple's three-week honeymoon, filled with sunshine, sea, and new experiences was thoroughly enjoyed by both of them.

CHAPTER TWENTY FIVE

Seated at the breakfast table, Roger switched on the T.V. News. It was the 2nd of April, 1982. He frowned as he listened intently to what the newscaster was saying:

ARGENTINA HAS INVADED AND OCCUPIED THE FALKLAND ISLANDS."

He almost choked on his cup of tea. He turned. "Good God, Belinda, Maggie Thatcher won't take that lying down." he said. "There are 1,800 people of British stock living there. Evidently, the small garrison of Royal Marines at Port Stanley tried to resist, but to no avail. They'll be trouble, you'll see. She might be our first female Prime Minister, but there is very little softness about her character, they are beginning to call her the 'Iron Lady'. She'll have our Army, Navy and Air Force teaching the Argentina's a lesson they won't forget in no time at all."

"Where is these Falkland islands; I've never heard of them?"

"They are a remote UK colony in the South Atlantic. War again! As if we've not had enough of it. When will they ever learn that there are no winners in war – everyone, is a loser."

Buttering a slice of toast, Belinda lay down her knife. "You mean there'll be a war? It's as serious as that!"

"Sure to be."

"Will John have to go to the Falklands?"

"I should imagine so. He is a regular."

She nodded. "He will be all right though, won't he?"

"Yes," he said, struggling to keep his own spirits up as well as hers. "He's an experienced pilot, he has been to other 'hot' spots and come back unscathed."

But despite his brave words; thinking of John and all he would have to face before very long brought back to him all the horror of war in the nineteen-forties, with his personal loss of so many good friends that he had known in Bomber Command.

As the days passed they avidly watched every news broadcast, learning from them that all this trouble was because the Argentina's asserted that the islands, the Falklands, South Georgia and the Sandwich Islands belonged to them, and had been their territory since the 19th Century. The British though, saw this occupation as an invasion of the territory that they considered theirs, also since the 19th Century.

On the 5th of April, the British Government, despatched a naval task force to engage the Argentinian Navy and Air Force before making an amphibious assault to the islands.

* * *

Within a few days, John, now aged thirty-six arrived in the islands with the other pilots of his squadron to help defend the British fleet, amongst them, the RFA Sir Galahad, which was bombed and set on fire by the Argentine Sky Hawk fighters during the Bluff Cove Air Attack. Other ships involved at that time were RFA Sir Lancelot, Sir Geraint, and Sir Percival, and many more. The destroyer, the HMS Sheffield was lost to fire on the 4th of May. She sank on the 10th of May.

John flew a Sea Harrier, these were informally known as 'Sha'. The Sea Harriers shot down twenty enemy aircraft, with only one of the Sea Harriers being lost to enemy fire; that one, unfortunately, being the one that John himself was flying. Hit by gunfire, his Harrier burst into flames. With the aid of a parachute, John managed to escape, but only just in time. Leaping from the plane, despite the throbbing pain in his right hand, he pulled on the cord attached to his parachute. Nothing happened. Unable to bear the pain in his right hand, he pulled at the cord again, this time with his left hand. Still nothing. He panicked. Was he about to die? His whole life seemed to move swiftly passed before his eyes.

At last, to his relief, with another sharp tug the

parachute opened and he sailed down to land safely in a field, just outside Port Stanley, the capital of the Falklands. He was found by some of his squadron and taken to safety. But John's face and right hand had been badly burnt – he was in agony. He was told that he would be sent back to the U.K, and to the Cromwell Hospital in London, where they had being doing plastic surgery since the 1940's. At that time, the plastic surgeon was Archibald McIndoe, who had been born in 1900 in Duneden in New Zealand. When WW11 broke out, he had moved to the recently rebuilt Queen Victoria Hospital in East Grinstead, Sussex, where he founded a centre for Plastic and Jaw surgery. There he treated very deep burns and serious facial disfigurements. Patients at the hospital joined the famous Guinea Pig club. After the war, he returned to private practice. His specialty was the McIndoe nose. He'd died of a heart attack in 1960.

John arrived at the Cromwell Hospital. He was deeply distressed, as well as being in a great deal of pain. This Argentine war had only lasted for 74 days. It had ended with the Argentina's surrender om the 14th of June. But in that time, his whole life had been ruined. What woman would want him now, disfigured as he was? He avoided mirrors, he couldn't face seeing the gargoyle that he had no doubt become.

The name of the plastic surgeon, a man in his fifties, who would be rebuilding his face and right hand was Thomas Bristol. But before this could happen, John suddenly developed an infection. He was very ill; not really expected to survive.

* * *

John's family were notified of this and they all arrived post-haste. They sat around the bed hoping that he would soon regain consciousness.

"He will come round, won't he, Dad?" asked Susan.

"We must keep hoping."

At this, Belinda began to cry and fumbled in her

handbag for her handkerchief. "He was such a lovely little boy," she mumbled, her nose buried in the depths of it.

Not always, Susan thought wryly, remembering his attitude to her at one time. Though that was all in the past, these days you'd have to go a long way to find a brother that was more caring than John. And he'd do anything for her two boys, Joe, aged nine, and five-year old Simon. As this was an emergency, Victor was looking after the children for her so she would be free to come to London with her parents to support them.

Roger put a comforting arm around Belinda, "Now come on; keep your pecker up. John's made of tough stuff. He'll come through this, you'll see."

This waiting, hoping and praying went on for several days.

One morning, though, Susan noticed a muscle moving in John's throat. "I think he's going to wake up. Ring the bell for the nurse."

Roger immediately did so.

At that moment, John opened his eyes. "Why are you all here, and looking so serious, too?"

The young nurse appeared and examined him. She smiled and turned to his waiting family. "Looks like he's on the mend. We'll know more when the doctor has seen him."

The doctor passed him AI. "We should be able to start on his plastic surgery treatment before very long."

This he did. Skin was taken from John's shoulder and used to make eyelids. His nose was grafted on in a later operation. He was given saline baths to help the healing process.

But when John looked into the mirror, he grimaced. What a sight he looked. He thought of the pretty young nurse who cared for him. She was called Pansy. With her golden hair and pink-and-white complexion she reminded him of a flower. He knew he had begun to get feelings for her. What a waste of time. With him looking like Frankenstein, no woman would ever fancy him again. But he was wrong.

They were seated together in the grounds of the Cromwell Hospital. It was a beautiful, summer's day in July 1983. Before them were bright flower beds and a luscious green lawn. Birds were singing in the trees overhead. Life seemed good. He eyed Pansy surreptitiously. She was so beautiful. .If only he wasn't so ugly.

All of sudden, she leant towards him, and to his astonishment, kissed him gently on the lips. He couldn't help himself, he responded, and kissed her back. The kiss lengthened. "I love you," he whispered.

I love you, too," she replied.

John frowned. "How can you, with me looking like a freak?"

"Well, I do. Anyway, you're not a freak. You're too hard on yourself. Your looks aren't as bad as you imagine. Anyway, *I go* for the person's personality, not their looks."

"Do you mean that?"

"I do."

He grinned. "Would you say 'I do' in front of the altar?

"I do, I do, I do," she replied, "and the sooner the better."

They were married a few weeks later.

CHAPTER TWENTY SIX

In 1985, Roger retired from the estate agents. He seemed to be at rather a loose end. He wasn't much of a gardener, not like his dad, the late George Bowler, and there was only so much watching T.V. or reading that he could do. Belinda got somewhat fed up with him always under her feet. She didn't want him tagging behind her everywhere she went, she had her women friends that she liked to go out with.

She came in from hanging out the washing to see him dozing in his armchair, a novel open on his lap. She nudged him. "Haven't you got anything better to do than to spend your days sleeping?"

"I run the hoover round for you once a week, and dry when you wash up – what more do you want?" he replied belligerently.

"For you to do something that will stretch you a bit."

"What do you suggest?"

She thought for a bit. "I know, why not write your autobiography? All about your time in Bomber Command during the war. I'm sure you'd enjoy reliving your experiences as you write."

"Maybe, but I don't know anything about the craft of writing."

"You could learn. You could join a writing class. I believe they run one at the Technical in Oxford. Why don't you try to find out? Have a look in the 'Oxford Times', see if any classes are being held at the moment."

So eventually, after quite a bit of nagging, Roger did just that. The writing class he found was held just once a week on a Tuesday evening at a local school, just off the Cowley Road. He went and found that he enjoyed it. Entering the room for the first time, he felt that he was back in school again seeing all the uniform rows of wooden desks. Apart from doing the writing exercises he met some interesting people – a few of them were already

185

published authors, but were taking the class as a refresher course. Taking the tutor, Miss Penworthy's advice, he got himself a Writing magazine and found the details of a Distance Learning course in Creative Writing. This course produced several short stories, which when he read them to his evening class members were highly acclaimed by them.

Next, he contacted Radio Oxford. He was thrilled when he was invited to read one of his stories on the programme. At this, he felt he was ready to start writing his autobiography. As advised by Miss Penworthy, he first wrote out a chapter plan. He had previously bought himself a word processor. It took a little while to master it, but eventually, he did so. Then, studying his novel plan, he carefully turned each section into a chapter. First of all, he wrote his autobiography which he had decided to name, 'Above the Clouds', in longhand. Gaining confidence, he tried typing it in on the word processor. He was slow at this - it being only one finger at a time. All the same, his autobiography grew, and grew. He would read a section each night to Belinda. She was very encouraging, making him suggestions as how to improve the plot.

* * *

Meanwhile, life for John was very good! He now had two children, a boy called Leonard, and a girl, called Emma. They were doing well at school, which pleased him and Pansy. He, himself was busy giving talks about his experiences in the Falklands. He even gave one which was broadcast on Radio Oxford. He too, was involved with charity work like the famous Simon Weston for people who were disfigured by accidents or illness.

Susan, also, was doing well, designing wedding dresses for foreign royalty. She and Victor had also bought a five-bedroomed house in Boars Hill – they needing a bigger house so they could put up friends and relatives after the parties that they often gave.

Roger's book was finished. He had paid to have it professionally critiqued. In the Writer's and Artists' Year Book, he found the name and address of a literary agent, and sent off his manuscript to them. At first, it came back by return of post 'Thanks, but no thanks!' Eventually, he had some good feedback from one of them, which he worked on. At last, just as he was at the point of giving up trying to get published, an agent took him on, saying the manuscript thrilled him! A few weeks later, he heard from the highly acclaimed White & Green Publishers. They agreed to publish, 'Above the Clouds' for which he would receive an advance of a considerable sum. His book was published. He ended up giving a book signing in W.H. Smiths. At this, his cup overflowed! A barrel-full ran over, when 'Above the Clouds' was proclaimed a best seller, and he was advised to enter it for the Booker Prize. Though he never won it, this led to him being interviewed on radio and TV. After this, sales rocketed, making his bank account very healthy indeed.

CHAPTER TWENTY SEVEN

Everyone was excited about the Millennium – the year 2,000. Some people prophesised doom and gloom – said that aeroplanes would fall out of the sky; that trains would run off the rails; that computers would pack up altogether. Roger didn't believe this, he always looked on the bright side of life, as in the main, did Belinda.

As they waited for midnight to chime and the fireworks that John had purchased to be let off, he dwelt on all that had happened to him over the last eighty years. Several times it had looked that he wouldn't see tomorrow – let alone this Millennium; at that time in the 1940's, the year 2,000 was so far away in the future that it was impossible to imagine. There was the occasion, during the war when he had to take over from the pilot and land their Lancaster himself – and on an earlier mission to Germany the bomb doors had stuck and he'd had to prise them open. If he had lost his balance at that moment, he would have fallen out of the plane to certain death. There was also the time when their airfield had been bombed; that had been a near thing too. If he'd been killed on any of those occasions he wouldn't be here now – seated next to Belinda in John and Pansy's home, having eaten so much party food that he felt he'd not be hungry again for a week, and with a glass of Champers in his hand.

He thought too, about their Golden Wedding party on the 5th of May 1999 – fifty years since they'd renewed their wedding vows at the Baptist chapel. They'd thought it best to celebrate their Golden Wedding then and not earlier in 1992 – fifty years since they had stood before a Justice of the Peace in Belinda's parents' home in Alabama.

All the family had been present to wish them well. John and Pansy had arranged everything at their own home, probably they thought all the catering would be a bit much for Roger and Belinda at the respective ages of seventy nine and seventy five. He and Belinda had never really expected then to see the turn of the century. He thought of all the family and friends who, sadly were no longer able to see it in with them.

"Raise your glasses," said John, as on the TV Big Ben began to chime the hour. Everyone seated around Roger and Belinda began to count in unison, "one, two, three, four......twelve!"

A loud cheer went up. Everyone toasted each other with whatever was in their glasses and said, "A Happy New Year."

John went outside and lit the fireworks. Through the window, everyone saw a shower of brightly coloured sparks light up the night sky.

He returned. "Come on. Up you all get. Let's sing 'Auld Lang Syne'."

Everyone rose to their feet, and linking arms and sang the traditional song at the tops of their voices.

"Should auld acquaintance be forgot
And never brought to mind?
Should auld acquaintance be forgot
And auld lang syne.

For auld lang syne, my jo,
For auld lang syne,
We'll take a cup
For auld lang syne."

Belinda, slightly out of breath sank back down on her chair. She thought of all that had happened to her in the past – her first wedding to Roger on the farm in Alabama. The terrifying time when the ship she was coming to England on was torpedoed by the Germans, then sunk. That ten days in the lifeboat with hardly any food or water, the meeting with Hank. She supposed she'd had a soft spot for him. She thought of the tornado that had blown her and Hank, and the wooden house away. Had he survived the tornado? If so, was he still alive and like herself toasting in the year 2,000?

Then there was the time in 1944 that they were caught in an air raid in London, just after Roger had received his medal from King George V1. That too, had been a near thing. If they'd not got into the Underground in time, well! She should be glad to still be alive, but somehow, she felt a little sad, she didn't know why. Was it because she was now old and couldn't expect to live much longer, or was it because she was afraid to lose Roger? Though she shouldn't really grumble, only having a few aches and pains at the age of seventy six.

She yawned. It was a job keeping up with the young ones .She had to admit she'd not be sorry to see her bed. She looked at Roger beside her, he too, was yawning. John, having noticed this came over to them. "Is it time to go, Mum and Dad?"

"Please," said Belinda. "I am tired, and I think your dad is too."

He helped them to their feet, and after saying, "goodnight," to everyone, accompanied by John, they went out to his car.

As he drove them to their house, passing so many others houses with brightly lit-up windows, revealing merrymakers, many of whom were jiving, Belinda heard the loud bangs and saw the showers of coloured sparks lighting up the night sky – making this night, a night to remember.

CHAPTER TWENTY EIGHT

It was 2010. The phone rang. He picked up the receiver. "Hello, Roger Bowler, speaking."

From the other end of the line came a familiar voice. It was Susan's eldest son, Joe. "Hi, Granddad, how are you and Grandma keeping?"

"Hello, Joe, we're fine. How are you keeping?"

"Great, Granddad. Never better. I've got a new girlfriend – she's lovely, a real beauty, and clever too. Can I bring her to meet you and Grandma?"

"Meet us! Of course, you don't need to ask. We'll be thrilled to meet her. So it's serious, is it?

"It is. I've bought her a ring. She's just moved in with me. We're saving up to get married."

Moved in, he thought. How different things were to when he was young. Then, a girl would have lost her good name if she'd lived with a man before marriage.. "I suppose weddings are expensive these days. Look, if you want a bit of financial help when you decide on the date, come to me."

"That's very good of you, Granddad. I'll bear it in mind."

"You do that."

"So when would it be convenient for me and Scarlett to visit?"

"Scarlett, that's a pretty name."

"Yes, it just suits her. So when shall we come?"

"Anytime, your gran and I don't socialize so much these days. How about next Tuesday evening? I suppose Scarlett works during the day?"

"Yes, she's a solicitor."

"You could come for a meal if you like?"

"Lovely, Granddad. What time?"

"Shall we say about seven pm?"

"That's arranged then Granddad, expect us next Tuesday, just before seven. Goodbye, Granddad."

"Goodbye, Joe." Roger replaced the receiver and turned to Belinda who had entered the room. "You got the gist of that, didn't you?"

"Sure did, hon,"

"It'll be great to see our Joe again. It's been some time, hasn't it? I wonder if this girl will be all that Joe says that she is."

"We'll find that out next Tuesday. I'd better decide what to do for the meal."

"You'll think of something tasty. Perhaps I should get a bottle of Champers to toast the newly engaged couple with?"

"Good idea, hon. I'd best find out my best crystal glasses.

* * *

The doorbell rang.

"That'll be them," said Roger to Belinda.

She nodded.

She looks a treat, thought Roger. Belinda had dressed in a pale green evening dress for the special occasion which she rarely wore, but that looked exceedingly good on her still slim figure. In her ears she had pretty silver dangling earrings that matched the silver embroidery on the dress. She had cajoled him into putting on his black velvet dinner jacket and green bowtie.

Everything was ready for the visitors. The table in the dining room was laid attractively with flowers and lit candles, which twinkled with golden light over the crystal glassware. In the oven, a large joint of beef roasted slowly. And in the fridge, were crystal dishes containing Belinda's speciality, her fruit trifle laced with sherry.

He opened the front door, and gasped. The girl with Joe was very pretty, it was true, and certainly smartly dressed, but she had tight black curls, and her thick lips were extenuated by bright red lipstick. Good God! This girlfriend of Joe's, was a Negro! What on earth would

Belinda think of that? She was from Alabama where the Negroes had been looked down on for generations by the 'whites', and certainly never socialized with.

"This is Scarlett, Granddad," said Joe, introducing her.

He took the hand she offered and shook it awkwardly. "You'd best come in," he stammered. He led the way into the dining room where Belinda was waiting. Joe didn't seem to register his stilted manner, but then probably he wouldn't! The young people in this country nowadays accepted people with dark skins easily, thought nothing of it, but how would Belinda react, having been brought up as she had? They could be in for a very embarrassing evening.

Entering the room he saw Belinda's eyes widen with shock, and when Scarlett came over and offered her hand, saying, "Pleased to meet you, Mrs Bowler."

Belinda mumbled something in reply and reluctantly took the hand, then dropped it quickly again after a half-heated handshake as if it had burnt her.

The meal and the wine were delicious. But the conversation was stilted and a lot of food was left on the plates by all concerned. Roger was relieved when Joe and Scarlett, feeling that something wasn't quite right, hastily made their excuses as to being tired after a hard day and left.

Belinda carried the used crockery into the kitchen. She turned to Roger who had followed her in with the glassware. "Joe can't marry her!"

"She seems a nice girl."

"She might be nice, but she's also a Negro. She just isn't a suitable match!"

"Isn't that up to him?"

"My mother would turn in her grave if she knew that I might be obliged to entertain a Negro in my house."

Roger thought back to when he'd first gone to America and been, not only shocked to see so many black faces, but also how the black Americans were treated by the white Americans; how they considered them second-class citizens. He'd excused such treatment then, thinking that perhaps it was okay, that perhaps it was all they deserved, recalling films he had seen where Negroes had captured white missionaries and put them in their cooking pots – he realised now that this was unlikely, and no doubt thought up by 'Hollywood'. "Look, Belinda," he said firmly, "that was Alabama and then, this is England, and now. The Twenty-first Century. The majority of people don't think like you do. You've got to change with the times."

"I can't!"

Roger sighed. This situation reminded him of the time his mother had made such a fuss about his brother, Wilfred marrying someone who'd had a baby when unmarried with a married man. She had eventually comes to terms with that, in fact, eventually she and Janet had become the best of friends. Though probably the problem of 'Colour Prejudice' was far more serious.

"Not only that," continued Belinda, "if and when he marries her their babies will be Piccaninays. They'd better not expect me to do any babysitting."

Roger frowned. "I'm sure they won't. They'll think you're too old anyway at eighty-six to leave with their children."

She glared at him. "There's no need to rub it in that I'm not as young as I used to be. I'm going to bed, I'll clear all this up in the morning."

"Suit yourself. I could put the crockery and glassware into the dishwasher for you."

"Don't you dare, I don't want everything smashed." With that she stormed off.

Roger heard her footsteps on the stairs. He hoped she would calm down and eventually accept the situation. Whom Joe married was his own business and no one else's.

* * *

Joe and Scarlett married six months later. Belinda, as

Roger had expected, refused to attend the ceremony and he had to go on his own. This felt a little strange to him, but there was no way he could talk her into attending their grandson's big day. Susan had fruitlessly tried, too. He knew the deeply ingrained prejudice that obviously Belinda still felt wasn't really her fault. It was the way she had been brought up.

Eventually, Joe and Scarlett had two children. Fortunately the boy and girl, Jack and Glenys took after Joe and not Scarlett, much to Belinda's relief, but even so she didn't find it easy to recognise them as family members. But as time passed, she began to regret the gap in the relationship between Joe's family and themselves.

Belinda was seated looking at an old photograph album. She turned a page and saw a picture of Joe when he was about ten – at that age he had always been at their house or going on outings with them – he and his younger brother, Simon. Now, they hadn't seen Joe for some time. It was all her fault, she knew – it stemmed from when she'd made it obvious that she didn't welcome in their home his future wife, Scarlett. She'd no excuse really. She'd been brought up to look down on Negroes, but was that right? She'd always imagined (since her childhood) that this was because she'd been taught to think that way She remembered being told by one of her parents' friends when she'd wanted to play with a little Negro girl, the daughter of their housemaid. "You can't mix with them. We think of them as animals!"

This attitude she knew for a fact had rubbed off on her. But was it now time to forget all that?

She recalled her late mother-in-law, Agatha Bowler and how she'd not wanted Roger's brother, Wilfred to marry her sister-in-law, Janet, because she'd had an illegitimate child. Mrs Bowler had come round in time, and later on she and Janet had become the best of friends.

Her attitude to Scarlett had made things awkward for both Joe and Roger – Roger now feeling excluded from his grandson's life, and she couldn't blame Joe for siding with

Scarlett, for the slight he felt she'd suffered. Belinda made up her mind. She would ring Scarlett at her office. Try to apologise. Try to make things right between them. Would this work? She couldn't blame Scarlett if it didn't!

She found the phone book and looked up the number of Scarlett's office. She picked up the phone, trembling as she did so. No time like the present. She'd do it now. She dialled the number, her heart beating like a drum. What if Scarlett once she knew who was on the line refused to speak to her? It would serve her right, she knew.

She heard the phone ringing, then being picked up, and a woman asked whom she was calling.

"Can I speak to Mrs. Scarlett Black?"

"Who's speaking?"

"It's Belinda Bowler – her husband's grandmother."

"Just one moment," said the woman on the other end of the line.

Seconds later, she heard a very surprised Scarlett speaking. "Mrs Bowler," she said, "Is something wrong?"

"No, nothing like that. Look, I know my attitude to you hasn't been as good as it could have been from the first time we met. And, I know it's a big thing to ask; but I'd like things to be different. I'd like you and I to be friends."

"What!"

"I know it won't be easy to forgive me for how I treated you, but I want to put things right between us. "

"Why?"

"I hate this barrier that I've erected between us. Apart from anything else it isn't fair to Joe's granddad, or to Joe. Could we meet and talk this over further?"

There was silence for a moment or two.

"I suppose so, if you really want to."

"I do, more than anything. It's very important to me. Shall I come into Oxford and meet you one day this week? We could meet at the Cadena Café in Cornmarket. That's near to your office, isn't it?"

"Yes, it was.. But I'm afraid it was demolished in 1970."

"Was it? I didn't know, or maybe I've forgotten, I forget more than I remember these days. At my age, I suppose it's only to be expected. What a shame, it was lovely there, at one time we used to go quite often. We could still meet up, there must be another café along there somewhere."

"There is. A new one opened recently, The Rose Bush," said Scarlett."

"We could meet up there tomorrow lunch time, twelve noon, if that would be convenient for you?"

"It certainly would. Thank you so much for being so understanding."

"No need to thank me, Scarlett. It's me who should apologise to you."

"You don't need to."

"Look, I'm thinking of Joe's granddad as well as Joe. What this would mean to them if we could put behind us the way I acted towards you when we first met. I'll see you tomorrow at The Rose Bush. Goodbye."

Goodbye," said Scarlett.

Belinda heard the phone being put down.

She decided she wouldn't tell Roger anything about this in case it didn't come off. Tomorrow, Tuesday was a suitable day to meet Scarlett as Roger, as he always did every Tuesday would be off playing bowls with his friends and having his lunch as usual in the Club House.

The next morning, she caught the bus to Gloucester Green. She alighted and walked up George Street and into Cornmarket. The clock of the Saxon church, St Michael's of the Northgate chimed the hour. Her step quickened. She mustn't be late and start off on the wrong foot with Scarlett. She paused where the Cadena café had once been (there was now a high-class dress shop in its place) in the old days, as she approached it, she would always smell the wonderful coffee aroma that the café was famous for . She wondered what The Rose Bush's coffee would be like? It was hardly likely it would be up to the Cadena's standard, even if it was, she felt almost too nervous to drink

197

anything..

She entered the café, blinking at the gloom after the bright light outside. Readjusting, she saw that the café was half empty, the Formica tops of the several small tables, littered with used crockery and screwed-up paper serviettes. Her memory replaced the unattractive scene with one from the past, with tables in the Cadena covered by gaily-checked cloths, each with a three-tiered cake-stand, and on them, a selection of mouth-watering cakes and pastries, and crowded with ladies, of all ages, shapes and sizes who were being served by waitresses in black satin dresses, white lace aprons and matching caps.

She sighed. How nice it had been to see the waitresses dressed like that instead of the haphazard attire they mostly wore these days. She noticed Scarlett seated at one of the tables. She gave her a tentative smile. Would everything go all right? She hoped so. She approached her. "Good of you to come. I hoped you would, but I wasn't sure."

"I couldn't just not turn up," replied Scarlett hesitatingly.. "That would be rude."

At this, Belinda realised that Joe's wife was as apprehensive about the situation as she was herself.

Making an effort, Scarlett continued. "Would you like coffee or tea? And perhaps a current bun?"

"I'll have a cup of coffee, but I'm not sure I could eat anything," replied Belinda, nervously.

"Of course you could. I'm going to have a bun myself. Look, of course, I'm going to forgive you. I realise how hard it must be for you to accept me brought up as you were in Alabama."

"That's wonderful. I'm very grateful."

"No need to be grateful. I want it as much as you do," said Scarlett.

"If that's the case, would you and Joe, and the children, of course, come to us for another meal one evening? I promise things will be very different from that other time if you could be kind enough to do this."

Scarlett smiled, and taking hold of Belinda's hand, patted it. "Of course, we will. We'll be only too happy.
She beckoned the waitress over. "A current bun, and two coffees, please."

The waitress returned with a plate containing a current bun and a foil-wrapped pat of butter, plus two mugs of coffee. As Scarlett buttered and ate her bun, Belinda sipped the coffee that tasted rather wishy-washy in her opinion, but she was so happy that everything was at last going to be all right with the family, she didn't really care.

CHAPTER TWENTY NINE

7th of August, 2014.

As she and Roger left the house, Belinda Bowler glanced at her wedding photograph in its ornate frame that took pride of place on the mantelpiece. As these days, apart from the time they had almost fallen out about Joe and Scarlett's wedding, they always saw eye to eye. This meant the photo never got laid on its front, unlike the one that had got lost in the tornado. Upset about losing the photograph (for the second time) she had told her mother about its loss. She had contacted Belinda's senator uncle, Uncle Stan, who had taken the photograph in the first place. Luckily, he still had the negative and was able to develop and print another copy which was sent to her just after she and Roger had renewed their wedding vows. To think she'd had this replacement photo for over sixty years.

Her parents had been dead now for almost thirty years. Though they had managed a visit to see them in the 70's and 80's. Despite the passage of so much time, she still missed her mother's letters.

* * *

Roger Bowler's son, John, and his daughter, Susan, helped their parents into John's car. They were driving to Lincolnshire to attend the Royal Air Force Battle of Britain flight. Roger and Belinda's grandchildren and great-grandchildren would have liked to have accompanied them to this great occasion but they had to work. Roger was now aged ninety four, with white hair that resembled a monk's tonsure. His wife, Belinda was ninety, her light brown hair these days owed something to the hairdresser's tint. But they were both still sprightly for their age. Roger thought of his old friends, Lionel and

Charlie. What a pity they hadn't lived to see this day. Lionel had died at the age of seventy, in 1990, and Charlie, when he was eighty, in the year 2,000. He still could hardly believe they were no long around. His brothers', Wilfred and Alec, fortunately were long livers like himself. Wilfred was now eighty-nine, and Alec was eighty six. They too, were still hale and hearty, but both of their wives, Janet and Charlotte were now deceased. As was Alec and Charlotte's handicapped son, George. He had never been able to sit up, or walk, and had also died in 1990, aged thirty-seven. It was a happy release, as he was always in so much pain.

They were to spend the night before the Memorial Flight at a Travel Lodge. Reaching Lincolnshire, they booked into the Travel Lodge .The next day they were all up early. Roger dressed in his uniform and fastened the row of medals across his chest.

Belinda kissed his cheek. "You do look smart, Roger," she said.

"And you look as pretty as the day we met," he responded.

She laughed. "Flatterer!"

They drove to R.A.F. Coningby, Lincolnshire where the Memorial Flight was to take place. The younger personnel there shook Roger warmly by the hand before they showed him and his party to their seats in the stands erected for the occasion. These Lancaster's that were to fly overhead in a short while were the last two airworthy Lancaster Bombers who were doing a month long visit to England from the Canadian War Plane Heritage Museum Avro Lancaster. These flights were a special salute to the surviving veterans of Bomber Command.

A few moments later, everyone looked up as these planes flew over to cheers and loud applause. Roger wiped his eyes as he remembered so many good friends who had not survived the conflict – especially Ben.

Then he heard a voice behind him, a voice despite the passage of so much time, seemed familiar.

"Good God, Roger Bowler! I thought you were dead!"

Roger turned and tears of joy filled his eyes. "I thought you were dead too, Ben. That's what I was told when I tried to find out your whereabouts after the war."

"I was told that about you. I can't understand how the RAF managed to make such a blunder."

"Me neither." The two men hugged each other. Ben's handlebar moustache was now white instead of light brown, as was his hair, but his friendly manner was exactly the same as it always had been; and after Roger had introduced his family, everyone went off to the R.A.F. Mess, where Roger and Ben downed a pint or two as they filled each other in on how life had treated them since their last meeting.

All of a sudden, Ben said, "Have you been to see the memorial in London to our lads in Bomber Command? It is on the Victoria Embankment, north side of the River Thames, between the R.A.F. memorial and Westminster Bridge. It was unveiled by Prince Charles and the Duchess of Cornwall in 2005.

"I have seen it on the T.V., and I have been meaning to go to London to see it in person," said Roger, "why, have you been to see it?"

"I'm like you, only seen it on the television."

"Why don't we see it together?"

"Good idea. I'd like that. When could you go?"

"Any time," replied Roger.

And a few weeks later they met up in London at Paddington Station. Roger had travelled up accompanied by John, and Ben, from Reading, with one of his sons. - Jasper. When Roger had learnt that Ben lived in Reading, he had been astounded. To think that for so many years they had only lived a few miles from each other. It appeared that Ben, when he'd been demobbed in 1945 had trained as a chef, and until he was seventy-five, he had run his own restaurant. His wife, Greta was now unfortunately deceased, but he had five sons, ten grandsons, and three great-grandsons.

After a meal in a restaurant, they headed for the Victoria Embankment and the memorial that meant so much to both of them. It had turned out to be a lovely sunny day, which exactly matched their mood at being in the company of their old friends once more. Both men, with the help of sticks walked slowly around the memorial, admiring the bronze statues showing five airmen in their flying kit.

"They look so young," reflected Roger.

"We were," said Ben. "we were only boys."

"We never thought of ourselves as boys, we thought we were men!"

Ben gave a half smile. "That's true, well, we would think that then, wouldn't we, but whether we were men or boys, everyone had to grow up very quickly."

Roger looked again at the statues, in his mind's eye seeing all those young men whom he would never forget. "They were the bravest of the brave," he murmured, tears in his eyes.

Ben nodded. "But not just them, you and I, too, though unlike them we were so fortunate not to have been cheated out of the long and satisfying lives which we have both enjoyed with the chance of leaving behind descendants – three generations."

"I agree wholeheartedly," said Roger, patting Ben's shoulder.